HARM'S HUNGER

BAD IN BOOTS SERIES

P.T. MICHELLE
PATRICE MICHELLE

LIMITLESS INK PRESS, LLC

HARM'S HUNGER

BY P.T. MICHELLE AND PATRICE MICHELLE

BAD IN BOOTS Series
Reading Order

Harm's Hunger
Ty's Temptation
Colt's Choice
Josh's Justice

Note: Harm's Hunger is the only novella. All the other books are novel length. Every book in the series can be read as a stand alone story

Texas charm is hard to resist...

COPYRIGHT

This is a work of fiction. Any references to historical events, real people, or real locales are used fictitiously. Other names, characters, places and incidents are the product of the author's imagination, and any resemblance to actual events, locales or persons, living or dead, is entirely coincidental.

To stay informed when the next **P.T. Michelle** book will be released, join P.T.'s free newsletter http://bit.ly/11tqAQN

SUMMARY

Jena Hudson returns to Texas to finalize the sale of her deceased aunt's ranch to her neighbor. The last thing she expected was to find her very own sexy, rugged cowboy in Harmon Steel.

Harm and Jena forge a white hot connection, but he learned a long time ago that happy-ever-afters don't exist.

So, what's a girl to do when she finds out the man capable of fulfilling all her steamiest fantasies doesn't believe in a happy ending? Given the right set of circumstances, she'll create one for him.

The books in the BAD IN BOOTS series can be read as stand alone stories. Reading order of the BAD IN BOOTS series, which is best suited for mature readers:

1

_____

"What do you mean, you don't know where she is?"
Ty Hudson raised his voice and switched his cell
phone to his other ear. His dark brows drew together as he
rubbed the back of his neck. "Her flight was due in at three.
Did you call her cell?"

As Ty cast him an apologetic glance, Harm placed his
booted foot across his knee and leaned back in the seat.
Looked like he might be here a while.

"She probably forgot to turn it back on once her plane
landed. Check that she did actually get on the plane and call
me back. Appreciate it, Colt." He snapped the phone closed.
"Sorry about the delay, Mr. Steele. I know you're anxious to
get the papers signed and get back to your ranch, but my sister
owns half the property. We need her signature as well." He
ran a hand through his close-cropped hair. "I wish I knew
why our great aunt stipulated we handle the transaction in
person if we decided to sell the property."

Harm rose and placed his black Stetson on his head.

"Sally Tanner was a fine woman. I'm sure she had her reasons. I can hang out for a couple of hours." He patted the cell phone in his jean pocket. "You've got my number. Call me when you locate your sister."

As he walked toward the elevators, Harm wondered for the fiftieth time why Sally deeded the land to the Hudsons. They were from the east coast, used to city living, not ranching. Sally had been a great neighbor, letting him use a large portion of her property to rotate his cattle. She'd always claimed, "It's the Texan way, Harmon. You take care of my horses, I'll let you use the land." And it was as simple as that for Sally. He'd miss the older woman.

He pushed the button for the lobby, but just his luck, the elevator skipped right past it, descending to the basement level. When the elevator doors slid open, a set of long, shapely legs stepped into the elevator.

Maybe his luck was about to turn.

"Hi." The curvy blonde with crystal blue eyes flashed a brief smile before she pushed the eighth floor button.

She was wearing a skimpy two-piece candy apple red bikini, her hair and skin still wet from the hotel pool she'd obviously taken advantage of. He nodded and ran his fingers across the brim of his hat. "Ma'am."

She looked him up and down with a grin. "Ooh, a real live cowboy."

"Born and bred." He grinned back.

When the elevator stopped on the lobby floor, Harm was thankful no one was waiting to get on. He hit the Close Door button, fully intending to bask in this woman's beauty as long as he could. A lift of her eyebrow told him she noticed he didn't punch a button for a different floor. Only the eighth floor button was lit.

As the elevator started to ascend, Harm asked, "Not from around here, I take it?" He couldn't place her accent. Virginia maybe? She had the huskiest voice. It was so damn sexy he wanted to keep talking just to listen to her speak.

She gave a throaty laugh. "No. Just visiting."

As she glanced up at the elevator lights, he took a moment to enjoy her luscious curves. He'd guess she was somewhere in her mid-twenties; she obviously worked out. Not one ounce of fat graced her nicely built body. She looked to be about five-eight or nine. A nice fit for his six-foot-three frame. The first stirrings of arousal tightened his crotch when he noticed her hard nipples pressed against her wet top. He let his gaze drop to her flat stomach and firm thighs. Nice. He'd bet his last dollar she had an ass that begged to be squeezed. Unfortunately, her hands were crossed behind her back, holding a hand towel against her damp suit.

When the elevator stopped on the sixth floor but the doors didn't open, they both looked at each other. Harm shrugged, then punched the button for the eighth floor to get it going again. Nothing happened. He hit the Open Door button but the doors didn't budge.

Lifting the emergency handset, Harm dialed the front desk. Once he'd set the receiver back on its cradle, he tried to look apologetic, but felt an easy smile tugging his lips. He couldn't help it. Now he had a few more minutes with her. It would take the front desk at least fifteen minutes to find maintenance.

Putting his hands on the handrail, he leaned back against the wall. "Looks like you're stuck with me for a few."

She adopted the same position on the opposite wall with an accepting sigh. "Sit a spell and all that, huh?"

He chuckled. "Yeah, something like that. Where are you from?"

"Maryland."

"Here for long?"

She shook her head, eyes twinkling. "Not officially."

A long moment of silence ensued as they both assessed each other. She had a beautiful oval face with almond shaped eyes and eyebrows slightly darker than her honey-blonde hair. But it was her lips that drew his attention. Free of lipstick, her full, naturally rosy lips made him throb. Those lips were made for kissing.

Her unabashed gaze roamed his face and body while he spent time appreciating her full frontal view. Were her nipples large quarters or small dimes? He was dying to peel away her bathing su—her bikini top's front snap giving way instantly derailed his lurid thoughts. As the stretchy material snapped backward and her luscious breasts spilled out, Harm blinked in disbelief, and for a split second wondered if he was dreaming.

Her sharp, embarrassed intake of breath snapped him back to reality, and he averted his gaze, turning his head. When she faced the wall and made frustrated sounds while trying to get her suit back together, Harm tried not to grin. Dimes. Perfect, rose-tipped dimes.

"Um, excuse me. Would you mind doing me a favor?" She called over her shoulder.

He cleared his throat. "Sure, can I turn around?"

She exhaled a short laugh. "Yes, you'll have to in order to help me."

Harm turned and immediately saw her problem. One of the hooks had caught on the back of her bikini top and she wasn't able to reach it. When he touched her back in order to release the hook, the brief brush of his fingers against her soft skin only made him throb harder.

"Thanks." She let the towel drop so she could fix her top.

Holy shit! What a beautiful ass. He couldn't tear his gaze away from the firm round flesh that the barely there bikini framed like a perfect picture.

She faced him, her eyebrow arched. "Enjoy the view?"

"Hell, yes," he admitted before he thought better of it.

She didn't look angry, just amused. Shrugging, she picked up her towel. "I was trying to avoid that."

His lips quirked. "I figured as much." He hadn't moved away and now only a foot separated them. Her scent reminded him of a lazy afternoon by the lake—some of the best memories from years past.

She leaned back against the wall, putting her hands on the handrail for support. "You know, I—" Her bathing suit popped open again, exposing her breasts once more. "...am apparently going to keep flashing you," she gritted out, her cheeks turning as red as her suit as she dropped the towel once more to grab the errant fabric.

"Won't hear any complaints from me. Flash away." He gave his best roguish grin.

"Uh-huh," she said, while trying to snap the scraps of material closed.

At that moment, the elevator started moving and her sarcastic expression turned to panic. Nodding his understanding, Harm reached out and pulled the red emergency button to stop the elevator. When he turned back to her she looked about ready to spit nails.

"Can I help?"

Huffing, she threw her hands up. "Have at it." As he moved closer, she added, "The bikini top, I mean."

He chuckled as he tipped his hat back and picked up the scraps of cloth.

JENA COULDN'T HELP but stare at the tall, sexy cowboy as he bent close. The expression on his face was one of concentration as he tried to fix her bikini top. His hat made him look even taller, while his navy blue button down shirt fit his muscular chest to perfection, showing off his tanned skin.

As he inched closer, his jean-clad leg brushed hers, reminding her of her first reaction to seeing those lean hips hugged in faded denim. The material had lighter streaks at the bend of his legs, which drew her gaze to the well-proportioned bulge at the fly. And now his hot bod was an inch away. She closed her eyes as a wave of strong attraction coursed through her. Where was this coming from? She'd never reacted so fiercely before, especially to someone she didn't know.

Once she tamped down her raging hormones, she opened her eyes, only to have her gaze zero in on the light brown hair that peeked out beneath his black hat. Was it as soft as it looked? Did it curl just a bit? *Geez, this is ridiculous, Jena. The man's a complete stranger.* But she couldn't help herself.

Thick brows framed his to-die-for chocolate brown eyes. A straight nose and a strong jaw with a small cleft in his chin finished out his handsome face. Tiny lines appeared around his eyes when he smiled, making him look a little older than the early thirties she guessed him to be.

She'd never met a man who smelled as good as this one did. He brought to mind the fresh outdoors with a hint of spice mixed in. If this was what she'd been missing living in Maryland, she might just reconsider staying in Texas. She stared at his large hands, tanned from working outdoors. Broad-palmed and long-fingered. He had the sexiest hands she'd ever seen. What would it feel like to have his hard-working hands on her? She imagined the combination of rough and tender would be electrifying.

When his knuckles nudged the plump fullness of her breast, she involuntarily sucked in her breath. Shivers coursed through her, settling into a throbbing heat. At her gasp, he stopped his movements. His dark gaze met hers for a long moment, assessing her. Letting the cloth drop, he smiled as he slowly drew his finger along her throat to the hollow at to bottom of her neck.

"Ever fantasized about kissing a complete stranger in an elevator?"

Her heart crashed in her chest. Who hadn't had that one?

She tried to smile but couldn't manage the expression, her nerves were too revved up. "Yeah, but my fantasy featured a tall cowboy wearing a black Stetson. Know where I can find one?"

His grin widened as he put his hand on the wall above her head. Leaning close, he stared at her mouth, his lips a breath a way. "I aim to please."

Her lips quirked. His arrogance only revved her more. "I really hope you do."

He dipped his head, but his lips barely brushed against hers. When he gave her another barely-there kiss, she realized he was waiting for an invitation. Jena tried hard not to lean into his kiss. What'd she have to do, bare her breasts for him? Oh, yeah. She'd already done that. The third time he teased her, she reached up and knocked his hat off so she could run her fingers through his hair. Curving her hand around his neck, she pulled him closer and whispered, "Make this one count."

His sensual lips covered hers, and the very first stroke of his hot tongue sliding inside her mouth, tangling with hers, sent her blood pressure skyrocketing. She moaned into his mouth and wrapped her arms around his neck as he stepped into her, pressing his very impressive erection against her.

He kissed her with a possessive intensity she hadn't expected. It was dominant and demanding, as if they'd been lovers for years, and God help her...it was a killer turn on. The electrifying sensation scattered all the way through her body, making the bottom of her feet tingle.

While one hand splayed across her back drawing her closer, the other hand moved to her naked breast and plucked at her nipple, the rough skin on his fingers a perfect drag against the soft bud. As he kissed her jaw, he grated out, "Just how far does this fantasy of yours go?"

She couldn't believe how much he made her feel. The way he kissed her, his unfettered sensuality, with such primal, immediate intimacy, blew her away. "As far as you're willing to take it." Her sincere response turned to a gasp of pleasure when he wrapped his big hands around her back and lowered his head to close his mouth over her nipple. Sucking on the hard tip, he rubbed his thumbs on the plump sides of her breasts, then gently nipped at the pink skin with his teeth.

"Be careful what you ask. I'm a demanding bastard." His hot breath bathed her breast right before he captured her throbbing skin once more and sucked harder. Jena dug her fingers into his shoulders and closed her eyes, absorbing the electric pleasure he gave. When he moved to the other breast and gave it equal attention, she pressed closer and panted, "Don't stop."

He pressed a hot kiss to the inside curve of her breast as his hand trailed down her belly. "You're so soft. If this is a dream, I sure as hell don't want to wake up," he murmured against her flushed skin.

She gave a half-laugh. "Me either."

He kissed her again, his voice turning gruff as he slipped his hand into her bikini bottom. "That's all the permission I needed." At his last word, his finger slid past the bikini-cut curls and delved deep into her core.

"Oh God." She inhaled deeply at the delicious sensations engulfing her. "On the demanding thing," she breathed out, "I think you've met your match."

Chuckling, he kissed a path back to her breast and drew on the hardened tip at the same time he strummed her body like the cords on a guitar in need of tuning. Jena clutched his hard shoulders for support, arching against his hand. She'd never wanted this seductive song to end.

"How close are you, darlin'?" he asked as he played her with masterful purpose.

Her body started to quake and she tensed her muscles, ready to fly apart. "Very," she gasped.

Withdrawing his hand from her body, he slid his moist

fingers along her sensitive skin, idling her on a high rev. "You're so warm and wet, a sweet summer dream."

She gritted her teeth when she noted the devilish gleam in his eye. He was toying with her. "Listen, I—"

He pressed a couple of fingers back inside her, fast and hard. Her breath hitched and she sighed in pleasure at the rough invasion.

A cocky eyebrow shot up. "You were saying?"

"Noth—nothing." A haze of passion engulfed her as her entire body bowed, preparing to climax.

"I feel how close you are." Leaning in, he kissed a path from her neck to her ear where he whispered, "But I want you hotter," and withdrew his hand once more.

"Damn you," she hissed. She was so primed she started to finish the job herself.

He grabbed her wrist and yanked her hand away with a deep rumbling growl. "Oh, no you don't. You asked for a fantasy. I'm damn well going to be the person who's going to give it to you."

Edgy tension ebbed through her, yet his comment made her throb more than she ever remembered feeling in her life.

They stood there, glaring at one another.

Jena started to pull her wrist away, but he used his hold to tug her against his chest. Before she could push away, he reached for her thighs and lifted, wrapping her legs around his waist as he set her against the wall.

Capturing her lips with a hungry kiss, his rough hands clutched her close while he drove his erection as far into her as clothes would allow.

Jena gripped his shoulders and arched against him, tiny whimpers of pleasure escaping her lips.

"Despite the jeans, you're making this feel pretty good," he moaned against her mouth.

Jena laughed as she reached between them to yank at the buckle on his pants. He backed his hips off just a bit so she could unbutton the top button and slide her hand inside. Gripping the warm, rigid flesh, she touched the tip with her thumb, teasing him. She smiled when he groaned and rocked into her hand. As soon as his breathing turned ragged, she released her hold.

He lifted his head from kissing her neck and met her gaze, clearly frustrated.

"You need to be hotter," she mocked.

"Damn you."

"Now why does that sound familiar?" Her amusement died a fast death when he pushed two fingers inside her once more, then ground his erection against his hand, adding more pressure. Panting, she gyrated her hips as he rubbed his thumb against her swollen flesh.

"Live the fantasy, sweetheart," he murmured as his fingers found her trigger spot deep within, applying just the right amount of pressure.

Jena buried her fingers deep into his shoulders at his husky words. Sensations curled within her, clawing, begging to be released. As if he knew just what she needed, he shoved his entire body against her, his thick chest and his lean hips holding her up while he rocked against her, winding her body into a tight coil of raging need.

"Yes, oh God." She tightened her legs around him, countering his rhythmic movements. She'd just opened her mouth to scream, when he kissed her deeply, taking her breath away as he carried her through a thoroughly satisfying orgasm.

Once her spasms finally stopped, he lowered her feet to the floor and put his forehead on hers. Their breathing sawed in and out for what seemed like an eternity before he lifted his warm brown gaze to hers with a wry look.

"We're doing this a little backwards, but...nice to meet you..."

"Jena."

"Jena," he repeated and smiled. "Harm."

She smiled and reached down to slide her fingers along his jeans. "Now, about your—"

The phone on the wall started to ring, reminding her that this man had her so caught up, she'd forgotten they were in an elevator, possibly angering many hotel guests.

Harm looked over at the phone. "Rotten timing."

She couldn't help but grin. "At least for one of us."

"Rub it in why don't you?" He grumbled as he adjusted his pants, then retrieved his hat from the floor before pushing the button back in.

"I still have a problem." She tried to hold her bikini top closed while also holding the towel over her barely covered bottom, but wasn't being very successful. "I took a chance with the deserted pool, but there are several families on my floor."

He rubbed the scruff on his jaw, eyeing her. "Hmmm, I see what you mean."

The elevator stopped and sure enough, a family stood outside the elevator. Harm quickly pulled her against his side, grabbing her butt, towel and all.

"Afternoon, folks," he said in a friendly voice, then walked off the elevator with her as if it were perfectly normal for him to have a tight hold on her rear.

"Um, that wasn't exactly what I had in mind," she said, trying to pretend her face wasn't on fire from embarrassment.

"What?" He looked down at her. "You wanted me to shadow you or something?" He shook his head and squeezed her rear as he whispered in her ear. "Uh-uh, darlin'. This is a lot more fun. Your sweet ass was made to be grabbed and often."

2

As Jena opened her hotel room door, the room phone rang. Who would be calling her? No one knew she was here yet. Clutching her bathing suit top together, she walked over to the nightstand and picked up the phone. "Hello?"

"Why the hell haven't you answered your cell? And why didn't you tell me you were coming a day early? I was worried something happened to you."

"My battery is dead and there's a reason I didn't tell you. I came to sight-see." She cast a smile toward the cowboy who'd shut the door behind him, towel in hand.

"It may have taken us six months to finally come to Texas, but I want to get this over with. You've kept Mr. Steele waiting long enough. Get down to my room. I'm in 614."

"Now?" She sighed, looking regretfully at Mr. Knock-your-socks-off-with-more-to-come.

"Now."

"All right. You don't have to be so snappy. I'll be there in fifteen minutes."

Replacing the receiver, she felt warm hands settle on her shoulders. Harm gently squeezed and massaged her bare skin. God, he had a magic touch.

"Problem?"

She turned to face him. "No, just some business I need to take care of."

He sighed, disappointment evident. "Yeah, me too. I'm expecting a phone call." He ran a finger along her jaw, a sexy smile canting the corners of his mouth. "How long will you be here?"

His light touch sent goose bumps scattering across her skin. "I don't know yet. I may leave as early as tomorrow."

"If this has to be goodbye, I understand." Harm cupped her face in his big hands and brushed her lips with his. When he slid his hand through her hair to cup the back of her head and pull her against him, Jena opened her mouth, accepting his intimate kiss and wanting more.

"I know you have to go." Lifting his head, his regretful gaze, heated and intense, dropped to her breasts and then her belly, sliding down to her toes. "The rest of my day won't be near as adventurous," he said as he took a step back and touched his hat, then turned to leave.

How many men would just walk away? Had she stumbled across a true gentleman? Jena stepped up behind him and wrapped her arms around his waist. Dropping her hand to cover the hard outline in his pants, she said in her sexiest voice, "I wouldn't want you to leave empty-handed, Harm."

HARM STOPPED, frozen in place. His body felt like he'd ridden bareback for a week, yet he'd forced himself to walk away from her, lust still raging. Thank God he wouldn't have to.

She pressed her cheek against his back and slid her hand up and down his package. "I do have a few minutes that I could put to some very good use."

As Harm gave a low laugh and threw his hat in a chair by the table, Jena slipped out of her ruined bikini top, then unbuttoned his shirt. When his shirt was completely open, she moved to unbuckle his belt and the top button on his jeans. She didn't bother with the rest, just pulled the fabric and the buttons gave way.

Heat curled in his belly, tightening his balls against his body. Her aggressive nature turned him on. Damn, he couldn't remember wanting a woman this much. Not only were her lips kissable as hell, but they were full and firm—just the right kind for other activities. If she went down on him even half as well as she kissed, he'd be in heaven.

Jena pulled back the gaudy green and yellow floral bedspread, then pushed him onto the bed and made fast work of removing the rest of his clothes. When she settled next to him and lightly stroked his erection, his hips moved involuntarily, bucking against her hand. Her skin was so soft and all he could think about was touching her, hearing her sigh and burying himself as deep as he could into her sweet body. Before she could touch him again Harm yanked her across his chest, kissing her long and hard. She tasted like honey and lemons, reminding him again of the lake...and thirst-quenching sweet tea. He wanted to know what the rest of her tasted like. Too damn bad they didn't have all afternoon to discover each other.

Jena pushed away from him, *tsking,* "As much as I would like to continue kissing your sexy mouth, I have more pressing matters," she tightened her hold on him, "to take care of."

Harm chuckled and let her have free rein. When her mouth closed over him, he closed his eyes and groaned, rocking his hips, pressing his length further into her hot, wet mouth.

Her tongue slid around the sensitive tip as she sucked and slid her hand down to his balls, playing with him. When she moved and took one of his balls in her mouth, covering it, tasting it with her tongue while she stroked his full length, he almost lost it, but she looked up, tightened her hold and said, "Not yet, Harm."

As she took him fully in her mouth once more, he slid his hand under her bikini bottom, squeezing her fine ass, then ran his fingers up her spine and back. He cupped the back of her head, changing the pace of her movements, showing her just how he wanted it.

And, fuckin'-A, did she deliver. Jena opened her throat, taking his hardness as far into her mouth as she could, gripping him at the base and pumping him, priming him. Sweet Mary. "Jena," he warned, but she just took more of him further down her throat. Holy shit, he wanted to let go. He had to use his hold on her hair to pull her off of him as his body rocked with one of the best damn climaxes he'd had in a very long time.

Jena didn't stop moving her hand along his cock until he was completely spent, but she turned angry eyes his way when he was done. "Why did you pull me off you?"

What? Most women would be glad. Harm leaned on his elbow and met her gaze as she got up and threw him the towel. She was obviously pissed.

"Jena, I'm a complete stranger. You don't know anything about my sexual history."

"Is there something you want to tell me?" she shot back.

He shook his head. "I'm clean, but I thought it best to not take chances since you didn't know that at the time."

As he got dressed, she appeared to be weighing what he said. "Thanks for considering me, I suppose." She sounded disgruntled.

Shaking his head, he chuckled as he pulled her into his arms. "This is the damnedest conversation. We certainly don't seem to do things the conventional way, do we?"

She wrapped her arms around his waist, laughing. "That does appear to be the case."

Harm kissed the tip of her nose. "I know you have to go, but will you have dinner with me later?"

"Yes," she said, turning her gorgeous eyes his way as she tightened her hold on him.

Harm didn't want to release her. He had to make himself walk away, but he paused for the briefest of seconds when he reached the door and realized he didn't know her last name. Now would be a hell of a time to ask. He set his jaw. Her last name could be Timbuktu for all he cared. He loved the fact she was uninhibited with him, but had a decent side that cared about propriety. The look on her face when she realized families would see her half-naked was priceless. He wanted to know her passions in life, which social issues pushed her buttons and if puppies and kids were her downfall. Beyond the fact she jacked him up, he'd enjoyed their banter and her quick wit; he had a feeling they'd get along well. As soon as his business was taken care of, he'd take her to dinner and do his best to convince her to stay longer.

"Mr. Steele is on his way," Ty called out absently as Jena closed the door.

Her gaze slid to the other person in the room. "Hi, Colt. What are you doing here?" Jena asked her cousin. He sat in a chair against the wall, his cowboy hat resting on his knee.

Colt unfolded his tall frame from the chair, put his hat on his head, then pulled her into a bear hug. "It appears your brother sent me on a wild goose chase for you earlier." He set her back from him and looked her over. "Look at you. You're all grown up and no longer the tagalong little girl." His dark brows drew together as a stern expression crossed his handsome face. "But I see you never outgrew your fly-by-the-seat-of-your-pants ways, Jena Lee."

Jena sighed. Only the Tanner brothers still called her that. Colt and his two younger brothers, Cade and Mace had teased her mercilessly during the couple of summers she'd spent on her great aunt's Double D ranch. The Tanners' own ranch, The Lonestar, was only a few miles down the road.

"I see you're still ever-the-responsible-one, Colt," Jena teased back.

Colt grinned and touched the rim of his hat, his blue eyes crinkling in the corners. "We all have to be good at something."

Ty cleared his throat and settled in a chair at the desk. Once he flipped though the paperwork, he rubbed his square jaw, his vivid green eyes meeting his cousin's across the room. "Thanks for waiting while we settle this, Colt." He looked back down at the papers. "Why Sally insisted we not use an attorney, but handle this transaction ourselves is beyond me."

Colt settled back in his chair, chuckling. "I think she and her brother were definitely of like minds. The Lonestar's a perfect example."

Ty glanced up from looking at the deed. "Yeah, I couldn't believe it when I heard Uncle James didn't leave his half of the ranch to you. What do you think Marie will do with her half?"

Jena noticed the tightening of Colt's mouth before he shrugged, then laughed outright. "Uncle James certainly threw me for a loop. But I've got it all under control. I'm going to buy the land from his wife."

"How do you know she'd sell it to you?" Jena asked.

Colt grinned. "Marie's retired. She's at a point where she wants to enjoy life, not feel hemmed in by the responsibilities of running a rodeo ranch."

His gaze traveled between Jena and Ty. "Steele is a good man. I see him often at horse auctions. I'm happy Sally's land is going to him. He deserves it."

Smoothing the short skirt of her yellow linen sundress, Jena settled on the corner of the desk to pick up the deed to the property and house. "As for why Aunt Sally asked us to take care of this in person, I think she wanted us to come back to visit Texas, considering we haven't been here since we were kids."

Her brother snorted while he rolled up the sleeves of his blue cotton dress shirt. "I can do without the heat. I'll take Maryland weather any day."

Jena ran her finger along the desk's smooth surface. "I don't know. I think Texas has a certain appeal."

Ty jerked his gaze to hers. "What do you mean—"

A knock cut him off. Ty stood and walked over to the door. Opening it, he extended his hand. "Thanks for your patience, Mr. Steele."

The man walked into the room at the same time Jena looked up. Her stomach instantly bottomed out. Mr. Steele turned out to be her fantasy cowboy. Heat suffused her face and neck as she watched him shake Colt's hand and discuss his latest horse purchase. When he finally met her gaze, his never wavered or showed surprise, though she knew he had to be as shocked as she was. He damned-well better be!

"I'm sorry about the delay." Ty cut his eyes back to her. "But my sister is a bit of a free spirit at times."

Harm raised a thick eyebrow and a small smile tilted the corners on his sensual mouth. "You don't say?"

Jena collected her wits and extended her hand, a secret smile playing on her lips. "Yes, I like to take opportunities as they arise. Jena Hudson. Nice to meet you."

He grasped her hand in a firm grip and met her gaze head on. The blatant look in his eyes told her he approved of her not-so-wet look. "Harmon Steele, Miss Hudson. Pleasure's all mine."

Harm's warm hand and the double meaning in his eyes made heat pool between her legs. Jena hoped her brother and cousin didn't notice the flush she knew stained her cheeks. She withdrew her hand from his and took the seat at the desk, needing to put distance between herself and Mr. Too-sexy-for-his-own-good.

"Okay, let's get down to business," Ty said, picking up the

paperwork. "Jena, I've already signed my half of Sally's ranch and holdings over to Mr. Steele. We just need your signature."

Harm pulled a check out of his pocket and set it on the desk.

"I'm not signing the deed over," Jena said.

"What!" All three men said in unison, staring at her with incredulous expressions.

She nodded and sat back in the chair, folding her arms. "I haven't had a chance to visit Sally's place yet. I want to before I make my decision."

"Do you always make it a habit of getting what you want, Miss Hudson?" Harm's Texan accent only accentuated the steely edge in his voice.

The look in his eyes told her he wasn't happy. She stood and put her hands on the desk, leaning forward. "No, but I want the decision to be mine, not because people," she looked pointedly at all of the men, "made the decision for me."

Harm crossed his arms over his hard chest and stared at her, a muscle popping in his jaw.

Ty coughed. "Um, is there something I'm missing here?"

Jena straightened and smoothed a hand over her hair. "No. I just want to see the ranch, but after the forty-five minute trip from the airport yesterday, my rental car died. I haven't been in my room long enough to see if they'd called me back yet. Can I use your rental?"

"I don't have one. Colt picked me up and we're meeting Mace and Cade for drinks in an hour." Her brother glanced at his watch, then pressed his lips together in a thin line. Oh, boy. He was pissed too. Served him right for assuming she'd just sign the ranch away without asking her. Darn autocratic men. All her life men have been making decisions for her. First her dad until his death, then Ty took over with this whole property thing and now Harm expecting her to sign, no questions asked. It's about time they saw this girl has a mind of her own.

As she and her brother stared each other down, Harm's calm voice cut through their battle of wills. "I'll take you to Sally's place."

Jena met his gaze. "I'll rent a car."

"Storm's brewing." Harm jerked his head toward the window. "If you're going to head out there, you'll want to beat it."

Jena followed his line of sight. The sky had turned black and menacing, threatening rain. She debated his offer. She really wanted to see Sally's ranch again. It had been twenty years. And the storm was getting closer by the minute.

Her brother sighed. "Go on, Jena, let Mr. Steele—"

"Harm."

"...Harm take you to Sally's ranch, get this out of your system, and get back here to sign the papers."

"Fine." Jena grabbed her purse and eyed all three men. "But I'm not promising anything."

Harm turned on his heel and walked out. She followed, almost running to keep up with him. How had her best fantasy personified turn into her enemy so quickly?

As the elevator descended to the garage, she chanced a glance his way. He stared straight ahead, not once looking at her. That didn't sit well with Jena at all. Thirty minutes ago the man had had his hand down her swimsuit. Not to mention the fact he'd given her the best damn orgasm she'd ever had. And that was with his hand. She could only imagine how the rest of him would feel against her.

She clamped her legs to stop the ache that had started at her wayward thoughts. It looked like they wouldn't be continuing where they left off earlier, but she'd be damned it she'd let him give her the cold shoulder either.

When they entered the garage, she grabbed his arm, pulling him up short. Harm looked purposefully at her hand and then met her gaze with an impassive one.

"Hey, it's not personal, Harm."

He turned to her, his expression shuttered. "That land should belong to me. I'm offering a fair price for it, and you're standing in my way."

She let go of his arm. "For some reason I can't fathom, Sally left the ranch to Ty and me. The least one of us can do is go see it one last time. Can you understand that?"

He considered her for a moment, and then gave a curt nod before he walked toward his red Ford truck. Unlocking her side, he helped her into the cab and shut the door before climbing into the truck himself. Removing his hat and cell phone, he placed them on the seat between them then met her gaze. "It'll take us about thirty minutes to get to Sally's place. I'm hoping we'll beat the storm."

While Harm drove, Jena surreptitiously studied his strong profile. The man was just too good-looking for words. Why in the world wasn't he wearing a ring on his finger? Well, he was already pissed at her. No better time than the present to find out. "So, why aren't you married?"

He gripped the wheel tighter. "That's none of your damned business."

His rough tone didn't intimidate her. "Considering that

we've been somewhat intimate, I think that gives me the right."

"That hardly counts."

"Oh, so fly-by-the-elevator encounters are a common occurrence for you?"

He shot her a hard look. "No, I've never—"

"See, I *am* special." She flashed a quick smile and raised her eyebrow, waiting.

Harm set his jaw and stared at the road. For a minute she wondered if he was going to ignore her, but then he finally spoke, "I don't believe in happy-ever-after."

"Really? That's pretty cynical for a man who knows how to fantasize."

HARM CUT his eyes to her, a smartass smirk on his lips. "I didn't say I don't know about pleasure." He shrugged, looking back at the road. "Finding the perfect person to settle down with is a childish fantasy."

Jena snorted and shook her head. "Oh, Harm. If you don't have something to look forward to, what's the point?"

He didn't really know the answer to that, but before he had a chance to ask Jena about her single status, rain started falling in heavy sheets. He gripped the steering wheel tighter, concentrating on the road. Lightning slashed across the dark sky, illuminating the road ahead of them. Loud claps of thunder immediately followed. Wind whistled and buffeted the truck, rocking it back and forth.

He cast a glance at Jena as he turned onto the dirt road leading to Sally's ranch. She had a firm hold on the molded door handle, her bottom lip clutched in her teeth.

Damn, it was raining like a sonofabitch. He couldn't see more than two feet ahead of him. Good thing they were almost to Sally's place. Another flash of lightning splintered the sky, and Harm looked up in time to see a huge tree falling right in their path. He slammed on brakes and swerved to avoid the mass of limbs and leaves. The dirt road underneath the tires had turned to slippery muck, allowing no traction when the brakes locked the wheels.

The truck began to fishtail and slide toward the side of the road. As they suddenly pitched into a ditch, Harm's head slammed against the steering wheel with brutal force. Immediate pain followed, then blissful blackness.

"HARM? *HARM!*" He heard a woman's frantic voice calling to him, felt her warm hands on his face, his head, the back of his neck. Torrential rain pinged on something metal—was that the roof of his truck?—and thunder rolled in the background. All the loud sounds jackhammered on his aching head.

He opened his eyes and tried to lift his head from the seat. "Sonofabitch," he hissed out as pain lanced across his forehead.

The woman touched him again, concern written on her face. "Oh, God, Harm. You were out for about a minute. I was so worried. You're going to have a massive knot on your head." She held up two fingers. "How many fingers do you see?"

"Two."

She put up two more. "Now how many?"

"A dozen." She frowned and he tried to grin, but grimaced instead. "Just Joshing. Four."

She swatted at his shoulder. "Don't scare me like that. You could have a concussion."

Who was this gorgeous woman? She talked as if she was very familiar with him. Where was she from? Her accent told him she wasn't originally from Texas.

He rubbed his forehead and frowned. "There is one thing. Who are you?"

3

J ena frowned. "That's not funny. Now is not the time to be joking while we're sitting in a ditch."

He shook his head, his expression truly puzzled. Touching a strand of her hair, he tried to smile but winced instead. "Not to say I don't mind sharing close quarters with you and all. Beats sitting in this rainstorm by myself. But I'm drawing a blank, darlin'."

Jena decided to avoid the subject for the time being. If he really did have amnesia, she didn't need to freak him out about that until after they'd reached Sally's house. If she remembered correctly, her ranch was just up the road.

She held up his smashed cell phone. "The crash made sure you won't be using this to call for help, but I believe the house is just up the road. Why don't we make a run for it, since the truck doesn't seem to be an option?"

He grabbed her arm before she could unbuckle herself and get out of the cab. "You didn't answer my question."

"How about we talk about it once we're under a roof, okay?" she said, trying to pull away.

"No. I know we're not far from Sally's ranch. Though I'm not sure why we're on this road. I know my name is Harmon Steele and that Sally's my neighbor, but I'm drawing a blank as to how you fit in the picture. I'm not going anywhere until you tell me who you are."

He looked at her in bemusement; not an ounce of his earlier anger showed on his face.

God, how long does temporary amnesia last? Jena's heart thumped hard. Maybe giving him some hints would help. "We were on our way to your neighbor's house—"

"Are we on a date?" he offered, an expectant smile tilting his lips.

"We made plans to go to dinner," she hedged, "but then we had to run an errand."

His brow furrowed. "Why can't I remember you? I think I'd have a hard time forgetting your beautiful face."

"And yet it feels like I've known you forever," Jena murmured as she glanced away, trying to think how much deeper a hole she should dig. Avoidance was always a good option. Reaching for the handle, she opened the door. Gravity pulled the heavy panel out of her hand toward the ditch. "Let's go," she said as she climbed out of the truck, only to ever-so-gracefully crumple to the ground.

Cold, driving rain soaked through her linen dress in two seconds flat. Harm leaned over her seat and poked his head out. "You okay?"

She grimaced and tried to stand, then collapsed again, yelping as pain shot up her ankle. Before she could respond to his question, his arms were around her, lifting her against his strong chest.

"Come on, sweetheart, we need to get out of this rain."

Sweetheart. That sounded nice, especially with that southern drawl. Jena settled her arms around his neck, enjoying the play of muscles surrounding her body, the heat of his skin a wonderful contrast to the cool rain beating on her. It was a good thing he'd put his Stetson back on; the brim provided some shelter from the relentless downpour. She looked up into his face at the same time he looked down at her. God, he took her breath away. The man exuded sheer confidence in every movement he made. He was simply—magnetic.

Harm set her down on the porch, seemingly unaffected by carrying her hundred and twenty-five pound body the quarter mile hike up the driveway and across Sally's front lawn. *Yep, hard-working man, no doubt, and a considerate one, too,* she thought as he handed her the oversized purse she usually carried around. When he unlocked the door, she was surprised. "You have a key?"

"Yeah. I take care of Sally's horses and such. Now that she's passed on, I keep an eye on her place, too." He lifted her again and walked inside.

When he set her down and stepped away, Jena began to shiver uncontrollably. The closed up house felt colder than outside. She set her purse on the table and hugged herself as her teeth began to chatter. "*Brrr.* Why didn't you tell me Texas could get this c-c-c-cold?"

He met her gaze, completely perplexed. "We're dating, but you don't live here?"

He thinks we're dating? Oh, boy. Now I know where the expression "snowballing" came from. How do I get out of this without freaking him out? "Um, our relationship is a little complicated."

Harm's eyebrow shot up right before lightning lit up the room. He glanced outside, then back to her, white teeth flashing in the darkness. "There's an old saying in Texas: "'If you don't like the weather, wait around. It'll change.'"

Harm flipped the light switch. Nothing. "The storm must've knocked out the power," he said as he lifted the phone receiver. "Phone's dead, too." He walked over to the kitchen cabinets, then pulled down a lantern and some matches. Once it was lit, the lantern cast a warm glow throughout Sally's ranch house. Carrying the lantern, he set it down on an end table next to the couch.

Jena looked around as Harm squatted in front of the fireplace to build a fire. The place was just as she remembered it: a stone fireplace, a soft brown leather couch, matching side chairs, and a throw rug in woven earth tones spread out in front of the fireplace. The kitchen and dining area melted right into the living room, a bathroom and a bedroom exited to the right. It was a very small, very cozy house.

Harm tossed the cushions off the couch, then pulled open the foldout bed. As he straightened the white sheets and burgundy insulated covers that were still on it, she asked, "What are you doing?"

He approached her and quickly turned her away from him. "I'm trying to get us dry and warm," he said, yanking her dress's zipper down.

He moved faster than she could think to stay one step ahead. Jena clung to the material plastered to her skin when he tried to pull it off her body. "Can't we just use towels or something?"

He peeled the sodden dress all the way off. "Nope. Sally requested all her clothes, towels, and sheets be donated to charity when she died. All that's left is what's on this bed and the one in her bedroom." He paused for a second. "It surprises me that I can remember that, but I can't remember us."

Unsnapping her bra, his fingers lingered on her skin before he slipped the straps down her shoulders. "Nice panties," he commented, sliding his hands down her waist toward her underwear.

Jena quickly kicked off her shoes, then slipped her panties off herself. As she dove under the covers and heard him chuckle, she ground her teeth.

I can handle this. He's just trying to keep me from freezing to death. She snuggled into the warmth of the covers and watched Harm pull the chairs from the kitchen table closer to the fire, then hang her clothes over them to dry.

Her breath caught as he began to strip out of his own clothes. Strong, muscular arms surfaced along with broad shoulders and an equally impressive chest. Sure she'd seen it before, but now...in this new situation where they weren't on even ground, she felt like a voyeur. Light brown hair clung to his chest as it veed down to his sculpted abs and narrow hips. Her heart raced as he pulled off his boots and socks, then reached for the button on his jeans. As he released the first button, her entire body tensed in suspense. Was it so wrong to admire such a beautifully built body?

Jena looked up and saw his heated gaze on her. He wanted her to watch him. Her mouth went dry at the sight of his long, thick shaft that emerged as he pulled off his wet pants and underwear. He wanted her. She clenched her legs together and tried to think pure thoughts. She needed to stay focused. Taking several deep breaths helped.

When he turned to put his clothes on the chairs, she loved that his backside consisted of two perfectly sculpted balls of muscle. Jena closed her eyes, cutting off the appealing, yet distracting picture.

A few seconds passed and then the bed dipped as Harm climbed into it. She kept her eyes shut, facing the fire. Maybe he'll just take a nap. No, he can't take a nap. He might have a concussion. She needed to keep him awake. That's it...she'll get him talking about himself.

Jena jumped when he cupped her breast and used his hold to pull her back against his chest. "Mmmm, now this is my idea of getting warm," he purred into her ear before placing a kiss on her neck. "Sit up for a second, sweetheart."

Keep this platonic, Jena. It's different now that you two have a history, even if it is a short one. Pulling the covers around her naked breasts, she sat up, facing the fire. When Harm began to rub her wet hair with a towel, she turned back to him, eyes narrowed in suspicion. Could he be faking this whole amnesia thing? "I thought you said all the towels were donated."

Harm lifted the kitchen towel. "I remembered these. Your hair is soaking wet. Turn around so I can dry it."

Jena saw sincerity in his gaze. Either he was the best actor she'd ever seen, or he wasn't faking. He'd obviously taken the towel to his own hair because it stood up on his head, going in a zillion crazy directions. As she turned around, she wondered how the man could look even sexier with his hair tousled. It just wasn't fair. She didn't want to think how she looked in comparison.

As his strong fingers massaged her scalp through the thin towel, she leaned back into his hands and moaned. The surety of his touch, the warmth of the fire soaking into her skin; the stirring combination made her feel safe and cared for. Too bad none of it was real.

When Harm traced a finger down her spine, goose bumps appeared on her arms, making her shiver. "You have a beautiful body," he whispered at the same time he turned her around, his handsome face close. "Tell me about us." His brow creased. "Starting with your last name. It really bothers me that I can't remember."

She placed her hands on his hard chest, loving the feel of muscles underneath her fingers. "It's Jena Lee." *Lee* is *my second name. Keep him talking, Jena.* "We've had a kind of long-distance thing." *Very long distance.* "I live in Maryland, so we get together when circumstances allow." *Twice so far.* She tilted her head and smiled. "That's probably why you can't remember me. I'm not in-your-face every day of your life." *That couldn't be a truer statement.*

He shook his head, frowning. "I'd never settle for a getting-together-when-we-can relationship. I'm not into casual sex."

She snorted, but caught herself before she blurted out, "Elevator ring any bells?"

Harm's brown eyes narrowed. "I don't share. Ever, Jena."

The protective possessiveness that flashed through his eyes felt as if he was giving her fair warning. Jena couldn't help the pleased shiver that passed through her. If only they'd met under different circumstances. She touched his jaw. "Do you find it so hard to believe you'd think I was worth waiting for?" *Because you are exactly the kind of man I'd be willing to wait for. I want a man who loves one woman with his heart and soul and expects the same in return. My gut tells me those qualities exist behind the shield you hold up to the world. Who created all that cynicism you carry around?*

Harm glanced away and as his jaw tightened under her fingers, as if he were struggling with conflicting emotions, she realized he wasn't going to tell her. *Why can't I show him that there's at least one woman out there who's worthy?* She gulped over the lie she was about to tell, but now was an opportunity to give him the fantasy he seemed determined not to believe in. "You asked me to move to Texas. I told you I'd come for a while and we'd decide from there."

Harm's gaze jerked back to hers and several seconds of silence passed between them. While his expression quickly shifted from suspicion to surprise before slipping into an inscrutable mask, Jena's stomach did several somersaults. Had she totally ruined it?

Finally, Harm traced a finger down her cheek, a self-deprecating half smile pulling at the corner of his mouth. "My head hurts from trying to figure out why the hell I'd let you leave Texas in the first place. I must've been a horse's ass in certain areas or you'd have said yes as soon as I asked you to stay."

She chuckled at his arrogance. How could he manage to be both infuriating and irresistible? "Pretty sure of yourself, aren't you?"

He ran his fingers along her jaw line, and the roughened

feel of his hand stroking her so tenderly made her want to weep. He was being her very own fantasy man.

"This pull I feel when I'm with you is indescribable. If I asked you to move to Texas, then it was because I'd planned to ask you to marry me. Kicks me in the gut just thinking I'd go down that path, but I don't do anything in half measures. I'm an all-or-nothing man."

At that moment, thunder boomed as if punctuating his words and backing up his sincerity. Her heart contracted. *Marry him? How did this get out of hand so fast? And why would it kick him in the gut to think about marrying?* He seemed to truly believe what he said. But if she told him the truth now, he'd be beyond furious. That's the last thing he needed with a head injury. But damn if her heart didn't swell at his blunt honesty. The man had a way of turning her to mush and he wasn't even trying. Was it so wrong that for a little while at least she wanted to believe the fantasy that he really did feel that deeply for her?

Her lips trembled a little but she managed to speak. "How about for now we just focus on keeping you awake to make sure you don't have a concussion."

Harm scowled. "That's not an answer."

Her eyebrows shot up and a smirk tilted her lips. "Oh, was that you asking?"

When his frown deepened, she smiled to lighten the sudden tension between them. "Since your memory is on the fritz, let's keep you talking and alert."

His lips curved into a dangerous smile as he tugged on the sheet she had clutched around her. "I can think of something to keep my mind *and* body occupied."

"I'm serious, Harm." Jena tried to smack his hand away. "You could have a concussion."

He gripped the sheet and used his hold to pull her close. Deep brown eyes searched her face. "I apparently have some lost time to make up for."

"Harm—"

His warm mouth captured hers, drowning out any objections and scattering her intentions to keep her distance. It wasn't fair that he was such a good kisser. His warm lips drew her in, totally obliterating the outside world.

She melted into him, opening her mouth for a deeper kiss. His tongue caressed hers, mated with her while he pushed her back against the bed and peeled the sheet away. Cupping her breast, he pinched her nipple between his fingers, making her arch against him and moan into his mouth.

"All mine," he rasped against her lips. As his hard thigh pushed between her legs, he kissed his way down her jaw and neck before capturing her nipple into his hot, moist mouth.

"Harm," she sighed, pressing closer. "Please tell me you have a condom in your jeans."

His low laugh rumbled against her chest. "Two, as a matter of fact, but I want to save them for later." His tongue created a searing path down her stomach as his fingers slipped between her legs, where he found her wet slit and immediately plunged two fingers inside.

She called his name again as his aggressive invasion put her on the edge of an orgasm.

Harm slowed his pace, saying, "Not yet," as he kissed his way down her navel, pausing to lick the crease where her leg joined her body. She never thought of that spot as an erogenous zone, but he just proved that part of her body was very sensitive indeed. His hot mouth had her body primed for his dining pleasure so fast, Jena's head spun.

He settled between her legs and laved a hot path from the back of her knee up to her inner thigh, touching her intimate swollen skin, then he traced the same path on the other leg. She bucked as he got closer to her wet entrance, but he pressed her hips back down on the bed. "I want you wetter."

"I can't get much wetter," she panted.

His dark eyes met hers. "Yes, you can. I want you dripping, Jena. I want more of you to taste, more to enjoy."

His demanding nature and carnal intent set an ache coursing through her body, and Jena let her head fall back, giving in. "Touch me, Harm." And he did.

He slid his finger across all her sensitive places, not leaving a single tingling inch untouched. When he pressed on a particularly responsive spot, she arched her back and ground her teeth to keep from begging. *Holy Jamolie.* She'd never felt anything like that before. Lust surged, hot and heavy, curling through her system. A sinful look crossed his features as he applied more pressure. Jena gripped the sheets and was shocked to hear herself begging, "Taste me."

With a grunt of satisfaction, he dipped his head, then swiped his tongue across her throbbing entrance until he found the responsive bud.

When she almost bucked him off of her, he gave a low laugh and pressed her hips back down on the bed once more. "You're the damnedest filly. Sit still so I can love on you."

"I can't," she gasped as he slid a finger in her aching channel and pressed on her hot spot deep inside. Lifting her hips once more, she begged, "Now! It's too much, Harm, I can't wait."

He tilted her hips and devoured her as if he couldn't get enough. Jena didn't think she could get any hotter, but the man took her twenty degrees higher. Every stroke of his tongue, every rough rasp had her teetering on the edge of her orgasm.

"You taste so damned amazing. The perfect combination of sweet and primal," he groaned against her. "I swear I might lose it just from the taste of you," he growled right before he delved his tongue deep inside her.

"Don't you dare," she hissed as her hips lifted to meet his tongue's thrusts.

Harm pressed on her nub with his thumb, rubbing the aching bit of skin in small circles, then rasped, "Show me how much you like it, Jena. I want *more*."

"Harm!" she screamed as her climax exploded, sending vibration after vibration crashing within her. Harm pressed closer, lapping every last drop as if she was the finest dessert and he was determined to lick the bowl clean.

When she began to slow her movements, he leaned over, grabbed his jeans and pulled, sending the chair over on its side as the soggy pants clung to the furniture. Digging out a condom, he swiftly slipped it on, then braced himself above her as he settled between her legs.

Jena sucked in her breath when his hard fullness began to slide inside her. He pushed further, groaning as she contracted around him.

"You're so tight." Harm's voice sounded gravelly and raw. "Relax, sweetheart, accept me."

She breathed out slowly, focusing on relaxing and not the stretching of highly sensitized skin.

"Jena, honey, I can't...I have to..."

She lifted her hips and accepted his powerful thrust as he sank deep inside her, filling her up, taking possession. Jena couldn't help the gasp of fulfillment that escaped.

He stopped. "Are you okay?"

"Yes, don't stop," she sighed, canting her hips.

He bucked at her words, groaning as she intentionally clenched her muscles around him.

She put her hands on his shoulders and met his intense gaze. "Don't hold back."

Harm began to move within her, his breathing choppy and hard as he withdrew and drove home again and again.

"More," she urged, digging her fingers in his shoulders. And he obliged until the entire couch rocked with their movements. She gyrated her hips, moving her hands to cup his firm buttocks and pull him closer. "Harder."

"Demanding woman," he gritted out as he folded her legs. Pressing her thighs to her sides, he surged into her once, twice more.

He was the perfect length, his hardness creating wonderful friction within her. She screamed his name as her orgasm hit, flooding through her, rolling into another one as he continued his unrelenting pace until their bodies were spent.

Cupping her face, he kissed her hard, then eased back and looked at her as if he couldn't quite believe she was real. "You're not going back to Maryland."

Before she could reply, he rolled onto his back and pulled her with him, settling her against his chest.

Jena didn't respond to his assumption she'd consent to be his wife. For pity's sake the man wasn't in his right mind, yet she couldn't resist letting her own mind wander down that interesting path as she ran her hand over the glistening hair on his chest, wet from their exertions.

Laying her chin on his chest, she met his languid, melting gaze. "Tell me why you've shied away from marriage until now."

Harm stiffened under her, then glanced away. She wasn't about to let him avoid the truth. Not now. "If you're asking me to marry you, don't you think I deserve to know?"

Turning his gaze back to her, he combed his fingers through her damp hair, searching her face. "I thought my parents had a good marriage. They stayed busy with our ranch. Dad raised the cattle and went to the market; Mom did the bills and ran the household. I didn't realize how unhappy they were until I was in my late teens."

She thought about her own parents' rare arguments when she was little. How she'd love it if her father were still alive—he'd only been gone a year now—so her parents could get into another row over something silly. She knew her mother wished the same. "No marriage is perfect."

"What about when they both don't want it?"

Jena raised her eyebrows, to which his lips thinned in a grim look. "I was at the lake raising hell with a bunch of friends from school, when I overheard some kids talking about my parents' land. That's when I found out my dad married my mom for the farmland. And my mom only married him to inherit the land her father felt should be left to a man—he didn't have any sons. It was the only way she felt she'd ever get out from under her dad's controlling thumb."

What a sad story. Jena's heart squeezed. "I'm sorry. I didn't know."

Closing his eyes, Harm rubbed his thumb and forefinger

across the back of his eyelids with a heavy sigh. "I've seen firsthand what staying in a loveless marriage can do to two people." His eyes snapped open, his gaze full of conviction. "I didn't know if I'd ever find someone I'd be willing to spend the rest of my life with, but as much as I hate to see my parents unhappy, I respect their commitment to their vows, 'til death do they part. When I marry, it's for life."

"Ah, now I see," she said, moving to lay her head on his chest.

He grasped her chin. "Uh-uh. Your turn. Why did you come to Texas when I asked you to?"

Jena hesitated. Any answer she gave would be part truth, part wishful thinking, part pure fantasy. Not only was she in some major lust with this amazing man, but she also really liked him. She'd always trusted her instincts on first impressions, and because of his connection with Sally, she knew more about him. Yeah, he was sexy and adventurous, but his character—that fundamental core that made him the man he projected to the world—sucked her in. He was fair in his business dealings, a great neighbor to Sally, believed deeply in his convictions—a gentleman from his head to his heart. He deserved an honest answer.

"I felt a connection with you on a deeper level." She sighed, flipping her hand. "I tried to deny it, but no other guy has caught my attention the way you have. No one's been worth all this effort." *You have no idea how truthful the "effort" part is.* "I know that sounds silly."

"No, it doesn't." Harm shook his head. "I'd lost faith I'd ever meet someone who felt just as connected to me. As far as I'm concerned, the attraction, the respect, the loyalty and trust...it all has to be strong, and it sure as hell has to be equal." Squinting, he rubbed his forehead. "How did we meet?"

Trust? Respect? She definitely respected *him*, but would he believe her intentions were pure—that she hoped to show him it was okay to let someone in—when she'd made up their entire relationship? Swallowing the guilty lump in her throat, she was thinking again about how she wished they'd met under different circumstances when her gaze landed on the welt that had formed on his forehead. "You'll have a nasty bruise tomorrow. I'm pretty sure you have a mild concussion."

He snorted. "You sound like a doctor. Is that how we met? Did you stitch me up or something?"

Was he in constant need of stitches being a rancher? He only had one tiny scar on his chin that she'd seen. Apparently, he wasn't giving up on this memory-lane trip, but he'd at least given her an idea as to how they'd met. "Close. Well, kind of. I'm a nurse. That's how we met. I was here for a medical convention and a mutual friend introduced us."

His eyebrows rose. "Which friend?"

Rack your brain, Jena. Think, think, think. What names do you remember Sally mentioning? Joe? No. Jake? No. Jack. Yeah. Good 'ole Jack.

"Jack."

His brows drew together. "My foreman?"

Jena nodded. "He and my dad knew each other. My dad told me to stop by and visit him while I was here for the conference last fall."

"And that's how we met?" he concluded, brow furrowed.

"Yep, and the rest, as they say, is history."

Harm shook his head as if Jack was the last name he

expected her to say. Pulling her closer, he kissed the tip of her nose. "Remind me to give Jack a raise."

Laughing, she laid her cheek on his skin, soaking it all in: the warmth of the fire, the steady rise and fall of his chest, the relaxed thump-thump of his heart, the masculine smell that was all Harm. All the sensations lulled her. She grew up believing in fairytales, and this...this was heaven. If only it wasn't a fantasy of her own making.

4

Jena waited until Harm's breathing leveled off in sleep before she eased off of him. She'd give him an hour, then wake him to make sure his head was okay. After testing her ankle, she walked over to the window. The storm still raged outside, but with the fire blazing behind her, the house was cozy and warm.

Since her dad's job moved them around a lot, she'd lived all over the country. When she moved out on her own, she'd traveled around Europe a bit, just to show her parents how it felt to have their daughter flitting all over the globe. But there was something special about Boone, Texas. The picturesque green valleys and crystal clear streams that filtered off of the main river of Sweetwater beckoned her, yet it was more than just the scenery. That inexplicable pull was the very reason she'd wanted to see her aunt's place once more before she made her decision. As soon as she stepped into the house, the happy memories she had there came flooding back. Aunt Sally's home might be tiny, but it represented the promise of a place to stay and settle. She'd always felt like it might be possible here, but in the past, she'd written it off as childhood romanticizing. Not any more.

No matter what happened between Harm and her, she'd made up her mind. Harm could buy Ty's portion of the land and part of hers. She didn't need tons of acreage. That should be a fair arrangement for all concerned.

"What are you thinking about so deeply, darlin'?" Harm slid his arms around her waist, gathering her back against his hard chest. The deep timbre of his voice surrounded her, resonating all the way down her spine. Jena closed her eyes at the feel of his strong arms and his masculine scent invading her senses. "I thought you were asleep," she murmured.

He kissed her temple. "I was until I reached over and you weren't there."

He settled her into his tall frame, melding them together. The unmistakable hardness pressing against her bare bottom made hot moisture gather between her legs. The man had the most amazing effect on her. She couldn't seem to get enough of him.

"What are you looking for in a husband?"

Surprised by Harm's serious question, Jena crossed her arms over his, then snuggled even deeper into his warmth. Between her father, brother, and her cousins, the Tanner brothers, she'd been surrounded by domineering men all her life. As much as she loved all of them, she could empathize with Harm's mother wanting to break free from a father whose only form of parenting was total control.

Jena had to pick up and move at least eight times at her father's career's whim. Then, the only reason they'd stayed in Maryland was because that was where Ty had been accepted to college, and her father had wanted to stay close to him. Not once was she asked how she felt about settling in Maryland. "I want my husband to let me make my own decisions. I want him to respect my need to do so, even if he disagrees with my choices."

Harm placed a feather-light kiss on her neck. "What if there are times when your husband does know best?"

Jena stiffened and Harm tightened his hold, not letting her pull away as she intended. "He'll learn real fast, I make up my own mind."

"What if he's just as stubborn as you?" He slid his hand up her waist and cupped her breast, twirling the nipple with a leisurely roll of his fingers.

Jena sucked in her breath, amazed by the achy desire his touch roused. "Then we'll have problems," she exhaled, sounding breathless as she tried to keep a firm hold of rational thoughts.

Harm slid a hand down her abdomen, spearing his fingers through the bit of hair between her legs. Drawing his finger along her over-sensitized flesh in a slow, lingering rub, his voice lowered, "What if he's willing to compromise?"

Jena arched against his hand. Her breathing turned shallow as she lifted her arms and wrapped them around his neck. Thinking became very difficult when he circled his finger around her aroused bud. "Co...compromise?"

"Pick a number. One." He slid a finger inside her and she moaned. "No, two." He added another finger, creating pressure with the sensuous glide of his fingers, wet from her own arousal, rubbing in and out of her body. "Ah, I think three is the lucky number." When a third finger joined the other two, he cupped her mound, then used his hold to draw her back, locking her body against his. "Three times a year, your husband gets carte blanche on a unilateral decision that concerns you. He may or may not exercise his rights, depending on whether the situation warrants it. What do you say?"

When she didn't answer right away, his thumb made a small circle around the responsive bit of skin, never quite hitting it. Just enough to rev her up. Jena whimpered and rocked her hips, wanting to move, needing the release her body sought. "Only if I get three for him as well."

Harm's chuckle rumbled against her back. "Quite the negotiator, aren't you?"

"Yes," she said, barely able to think while wanting him to touch her, "and right now I'm ordering you to give me what I want."

"No, sweetheart, I'm going to give you what you *need*." He kissed the delicate skin behind her ear. "Me," he said in a husky tone as he stopped circling his thumb and honed in on the sensitive, aching skin, applying steady pressure. At the same time, his other hand clasped the plump flesh of her breast in a possessive hold.

"Harm..." She gulped. "That feels so good," she panted, rocking into his hand when he began to slide his fingers in and out of her body once more.

While plucking out a seductive, rhythmic tune against her taut frame, Harm didn't forget about the rest of her erogenous zones. He twirled her nipple, teasing the hard bud with just the right pinching-pressure. The combination of his actions sent Jena over the edge. Her body trembled through the force of her orgasm. She cried out as pure pleasure spiraled from her breasts to her stomach, to her thighs and beyond.

Once her heart rate slowed, she turned, only to have it speed right back up. She stared in fascination as she watched Harm suck her essence off each finger, one-by-one, rumbling his approval. Pure desire, in its most primal form, slammed into her stomach as she watched him savor her.

Decadent satisfaction had turned his eyes so dark brown, they almost looked black. Just as he started to speak, her stomach made a gurgling sound and Jena laughed to cover her embarrassment.

Harm glanced down at her belly, an apologetic look crossing his face. "Are you hungry? All I have to offer are apples and carrots." He gave an adorable, lopsided grin. "Horses love 'em as a treat."

She returned his smile with a knowing grin. "Yes, I'm hungry." Reaching out, she wrapped her fingers around his thick, rigid shaft, then raised her eyebrow suggestively as she ran her thumb over the drop of arousal moistening the tip.

Harm eyes blazed with smoldering heat. His gaze dropped to her lips, and his nostrils flared as a predatory smile quirked the corners of his lips. "Never say I don't know how to provide the most important food group for my woman."

His woman. That sounded just right to her. Jena pointed to the kitchen chair in front of the fireplace. "Go sit."

HARM GRINNED and followed her orders. He heard her rummaging around in her purse while he moved some wet clothes to another chair. Positioning the empty chair in front of the fire, he sat, waiting for Jena.

She was the most stimulating woman. Why in the world had he let their explosive relationship go on for months before he decided to do something about it? He didn't know what freight train finally had to hit him, but he was glad he came to his senses. His stomach tightened into knots when he realized his own stubborn convictions could have pushed this wonderful woman into another man's arms.

Harm clenched his jaw at the mere thought. She was his. Period. He'd never felt so strongly about another person. The tension in his chest, the gnawing feeling in his stomach, and the electricity coursing through him were throwing him off-balance. It all felt like some kind of surreal dream, one that he sure as hell didn't want to wake up from.

Jena's hand brushing over his shoulder drew him out of his reverie. Harm clasped her around the waist, intending to bury his face against her silky breasts. "Uh-uh." She pulled away and stood facing him. "No touching."

He raised an eyebrow. "Is that the way it's going to be?"

Nodding, she tapped her finger against her lips as she took a slow circle around the chair. The whole time she sized him up, a sexy smile played on her lips. Desire and mischief filled her gaze. She appeared to be deciding just what she wanted to do with him. Harm's cock throbbed against his belly. He was ready as hell.

She stopped in front of him once more and laid her hands on his thighs. When she slid them to the crease in his legs and touched his sac lightly with her thumbs, he couldn't stop the shudder that rippled through him. When she pushed his thighs further apart, Harm gritted his teeth to stay focused. The lightning lust that surged through his body at the mere thought of what she had in mind felt like he'd been punched in the balls. He lifted his hands to cup her breasts, but she backed away, shaking her head.

Now he understood. If he touched her at all, she'd stop. Harm set his jaw and clamped his hands on the bottom of the chair. Damn, it was the only way he'd keep from touching her. She was a gorgeous sight to behold, the fire reflecting off her peach-toned skin and honey-blonde hair made her appear ethereal—like his very own seductive angel. He ached to touch her just to see her cheeks flush with desire once more. Perfect breasts, more than a handful and ruby red nipples, jutted out impudently at him, teasing him, torturing him. He wanted to taste her so bad his mouth watered.

When she went down on her knees in front of him, Harm held back the howl of animal satisfaction that roared deep within his chest. Jena traced the inside of his thigh with her tongue until she reached his sac. His throat tightened when she flicked the ultra sensitive skin with the tip of her tongue. Harm's hips moved of their own accord, closer to her hot mouth. But she moved to his other leg and repeated the same process all over again until her mouth rested over him. Giving him a minx-like smile, she grasped his cock with one hand and fondled him with the other.

"Taste me, Jena." The request was out before he could stop himself.

She tortured him with her tongue once more, touching every ridge and crevice as she licked a path along the entire length of his erection. Harm's balls tightened in erotic antici-pation, and his stomach tensed as he waited for her mouth to surround him. He clenched his hands tight on the chair to keep from brushing his fingers along the curve of her spine, to feel her soft skin pebble from his touch. He gritted his teeth and tamped down the urge. Later, he promised himself.

When she closed her mouth over him, stroking his heightened skin with her tongue, the unexpected cool, tingling sensation nearly rocked his world. Harm took deep breaths to keep from coming too soon. He fucking wanted this fantasy to last. As she worked her mouth up and down his length, he managed to rasp out between building, coiling tension and ragged breaths, "What do you have in your mouth? It's incredible."

"Hmmm," she hummed her response and he bucked against her as the vibrating sensation spread like wildfire throughout his lower torso and thighs.

Harm gave into his natural inclination. Without thinking, he placed a hand on the crown of her head and directed her to take him further. Jena's eager accommodation to his silent request had him groaning his approval. As her sensual nature shook him to the core, an odd sense of déjà vu rocketed through him, making oral sex with Jena that much more exciting.

He lifted his hips and rocked against her hot, moist mouth, murmuring her name as she took a long, sucking drag. When she bit down, then circled his shaft with her tongue, as if soothing her love nip, pleasure-pain shot through him. On the brink of his orgasm, he held back, determined to prolong the thousand jolts of awareness that radiated throughout his body, yet centered with her talented tongue and kissable lips.

When he caught the scent of her own arousal and heard her moan, Harm was lost. A primal growl erupted as he let go, rocking hard against her warm mouth. The knowledge that Jena took everything he offered with pleasure made his orgasm one of the longest, most fulfilling climaxes he'd ever experienced.

The scent of mint surrounded him as she stood, leaned close and whispered, "strong peppermints," before kissing him deeply. He started to pull her into his lap, but she drew back with a wicked grin.

"You see, the reason I would even consider agreeing to your compromise is because I know who *really* wields all the power."

"Is that right?" Harm gave a cocky smile and before she could move away, he swiped his finger along her entrance, gathering the sweetness he knew awaited his touch. While she gasped her surprise that he knew how turned on she was, he raised an eyebrow and slid the wet finger into his mouth.

Pulling Jena between his legs, he captured her lips, his kiss intense and thorough. She sighed against his mouth, folding into his body. His heart skipped a beat with the knowledge that he felt so deeply for this woman it scared him. Those three chances were as much for his sanity as hers. Otherwise, she'd have him completely wrapped around her finger even more than he already was. He vowed to himself before the evening was out, he'd have Jena as addicted to him as he was to her.

Harm set her on the floor and pulled the chairs out of the way. "Wait here. I'll get us some food."

Jena watched the flex and play of his taut butt cheeks as he walked toward the kitchen. The display of muscles and naked male flesh made her weak in the knees. She couldn't believe how well they'd connected. What would he say when his memory came back? Would he despise her? Her stomach pitched.

Shaking her worried thoughts away, she vowed that if Harm didn't get his memory back by tomorrow, she'd tell him the truth. She didn't want to think about what might happen between them as a result. A crackle and hissing pop from the fire drew her attention. The heat felt so good against her skin. She touched her clothes and sighed. The material was still damp. While she waited for Harm, she stretched out on her belly across the rug and basked in the fire's warmth.

When the smell of apples invaded her senses, Jena lifted her head from her cradled arms. She smiled as Harm drew the apple slice away from her nose and popped it into his mouth. He'd apparently turned out the lantern, and the surrounding darkness made the glow of the firelight even more intimate.

"Hey, sleepyhead." Harm leaned back against the foldout bed and propped his elbow on his bent knee, totally at home with his nakedness in front of her.

Why did it seem perfectly natural to be lying here naked in front of him? Jena stretched and smiled. "Guess the fire put me right to sleep."

"Didn't have anything to do with your earlier exertions," he said, winking at her.

Damn, he was one sexy man. Jena chuckled and rose up on her elbows to take a slice of apple from the plate he'd set between them. "Oh, I suppose it might have something to do with that." She nibbled on the piece of fruit. "Your turn. Tell me what you're looking for in a wife."

He shifted his gaze to the fire as if the flames held the answer. "I want someone who accepts what I am—a rancher, no more, no less—who's willing to live that lifestyle with me. Someone who attracts me both mentally and physically." His eyes met hers. "Someone I can enjoy the give and take of debating with just as much as the give and take while making love..." Heat curled in her belly as Harm paused to rake his gaze across her naked back and buttocks. His dark eyes met hers as he continued, "And I've found her."

Jena swallowed the piece of apple that threatened to lodge in her throat. She rolled onto her side, propped up on her elbow and faced him. "Harm, all I said was that I would come and stay for a while."

Her heart raced as Harm pushed her on her back and leaned over her, his hands braced on the floor around her. "I thought I said this already. You're not going back to Maryland." He punctuated his words while kissing a path along her throat.

She pushed at his shoulders until he lifted his head. "And I told you I make my own decisions."

There was arrogance in his low laugh, but his expression was dead serious. "Didn't I tell you? I'm exercising my right at a unilateral decision on your behalf."

Jena laughed at his self-assured confidence. "But that was as my husband."

He raised an eyebrow. "As far as I'm concerned, it's a done deal. And as you know, I don't commit lightly."

"All the more reason for you to really think before you commit yourself." Panic clawed in her chest. *He's going to kill me when he gets his memory back. At the very least, he'll never forgive me.* Jena pushed at his arms, needing space. Harm leaned back and let her rise. The look on his face was so inscrutable she couldn't decipher what he was thinking.

Without a word, he stood and lifted her in his arms. Setting her on the bed, he climbed in behind her, then pulled her back until her butt rested against the cradle of his hips and thighs. As he settled his chest against her back, then splayed his hand across her belly in a you're-mine hold, Jena wished he'd never bumped his head, that she'd never set this whole fabricated fantasy in motion. But if she hadn't taken the reins with this whole amnesia thing, Harm would've felt vulnerable in a total stranger's presence. He would've held the most important parts of himself back, and she would never have gotten to know the real Harmon Steele.

"Don't move," Harm whispered in her ear. Jena surfaced from deep slumber when he laid his hot, naked body across her back. Pinned to the bed, her heart beat faster as he laced his fingers with hers, silently directing her to curl her hands around the mattress edge above her head.

Her skin prickled with sexual excitement as he slid his palms down her back to the indention of her waist. The fire had died to dull red embers, and the sound of rolling thunder sounded far off. Only an occasional flash of lightning illuminated the otherwise pitch-dark room.

Jena sucked in her breath when he lifted her hips. She started to rise up on her hands and knees, but Harm put a hand on her back, silently telling her to remain as she was— her butt tilted in the air, her face on the pillow, arms stretched above her, hands clutching the bed.

When he slid a finger inside her and slowly turned it around, finding and pressing on her g-spot, she bucked against his hand. His touch disappeared and she started to sit up and complain, but the sensation of his thumbs spreading her and his mouth finding just the right spot had her collapsing with a sigh of pleasure.

"I can't get enough of you," Harm murmured as he alternatively tugged at the tiny bud and laved her juices that gathered in response to his masterful manipulation.

Jena had never felt so achingly vulnerable and decadent in her life. She clutched the foldout mattress and rocked against him, raging need building inside her.

"The give and take, Jena, remember," he murmured against her body. He worked his fingers inside her until she was wet all over, then he traced every crevice with his tongue. Harm lingered, leisurely enjoying her body's natural response before he started the same process over. Again and again, he took her to the edge until her thighs trembled and her body quaked with need.

He was driving her insane. Only the occasional thrust of his tongue deep within her heated core or flicking against her aching nub marginally assuaged her building desire. Damn, he was skilled at oral sex. She'd never met a man who took the time to taste her—no, to *savor* her—as much as Harm did.

He slid a finger in her core once more, then planted a kiss on the curve of her rear and said in a serious tone, "Do you trust me, Jena?"

She was about out of her mind, her body screaming for release from the sinfully tortuous path he'd led her down. "Yes," she managed to say between pants. In her heart, she knew she did. Her pulse raced as she waited for Harm's response.

Harm pushed her thighs further apart and slipped something— What was that? A half piece of ice?—inside her. "Oh, God!" she cried out and rose up on her hands and knees as her entire core suddenly went from raging hot to freezing cold.

Cupping his hand over her entrance, Harm held her body closed while he slid his fingers back and forth against her clit, revving her higher. With one hand continuing to work against her sex, he laid his chest over her back and used his other hand to tweak her nipple. When his lips landed on her shoulder in a tender kiss, it was all she could do not to whimper.

"Let go, Jena. Let your sweet tasting body melt the ice the way you melt me."

Chill bumps rose on her skin, but the cold no longer existed. Only the hot, husky need in his voice and the pent-up tension remained. Jena moved with the motion of his hand, seeking fulfillment. She finally let out the whimper she'd been holding back and rocked, seeking to assuage the yearning need raging within her. But it wasn't until Harm pulled back and swiped his tongue in a long, reverent lick against her that she felt the first tremors of her orgasm take over. She moaned and tightened her body, preparing.

Before she shattered to pieces, Harm immediately sat on the bed and pulled her back against his chest. He let out a strained growl as he lowered her hips over his thighs and slid his cock inside her. Back to chest, soft thighs surrounding his rock hard ones, Jena gasped in sheer delight. Her muscles flexed as she lifted herself up and down, enjoying the hard fullness, taking her...possessing her, making her all his.

Harm slid his fingers between her legs and rasped as his

breathing turned labored, "The next time we make love, I'm not wearing a damn condom."

Jena sobbed as her body shuddered with the most powerful orgasm she'd ever experienced. He had ruined her for all men, for she knew without a doubt she was hopelessly addicted to this man's unquenchable hunger.

5

Harm awoke the next morning feeling stiff all over yet mentally rested. His head throbbed, but it didn't compare to the jerking of his heart when he saw Jena wasn't in bed. Her clothes were gone from the chairs as well. As he quickly dressed in his jeans, the phone rang. He dove for it, jamming his toe on the kitchen table in the process.

"Hello!" he growled as pain radiated throughout his foot.

"Harm?"

"Yeah?" He racked his brain, but the male voice on the other end of the line didn't sound familiar.

"It's Ty. I've been trying to reach you all night. Man, that was a hell of a storm last night. I'm assuming you and Jena stayed at Sally's place to ride it out. Did she make up her mind to sign the papers yet?"

Hell of a storm.

Sally's place

Sign the papers.

The phrases triggered Harm's memories. Like a drawbridge slowly being opened, the chain's links unwound from the wheel and they all came flooding back.

Jena in the elevator, then in her hotel room.

Jena's smile when he asked her to dinner.

Jena looking gorgeous and surprised when he walked into her brother's hotel room.

Jena refusing to sign her half of the ranch over to him.

Jena challenging him, making him think more than he wanted to during the trip to Sally's place.

The storm.

The wreck.

"Harm? You there? Did Jena sign?"

"Not yet. She'll give you a call back later."

Harm hung up before Ty could respond and took several deep breaths. He felt like he'd been kicked in the chest and racked in the balls for good measure.

JENA SIGHED HEAVILY and leaned over the fence to pat the horse's nose as the sun finally crested the sky. "Good morning, girl. Guess I've delayed long enough. Time to wake up Harm and tell him the truth."

Even though Harm had gotten up earlier to take care of the horses, he'd come back to bed and pulled her close before falling asleep once more. The simple act meant he hadn't regained his memory. As much as she craved the closeness, she'd been unable to fall back to sleep. The thought of waking up to the sun rising with Harm holding her so intimately made her heart ache. Last night had been amazing, but with the blush of the new day coming, her stomach knotted. She didn't want to tell Harm, didn't want to see his smile turn into a scowl or his eyes darken with anger.

Patting the horse once more, she made her way back to the house. As she walked in, she was surprised to see the sofa already put back together and Harm leaning against the kitchen table, his boots crossed. "Oh, hi. I didn't expect you to be up yet."

"When were you planning on telling me?" he said, his tone cold, hard.

Her stomach bottomed out. "When did your memory come back?" she asked in a quiet tone.

He jerked his head toward the phone. "When your brother called to check on us. When, Jena?" he snapped.

She stilled herself to keep from jumping at his fierce tone as she closed the door. "I was coming in to tell you just now."

He crossed his arms, his face turning to stone. "Go on, I can't wait to hear your explanation for why you lied? Why you gave us a past and planned our whole future?"

She gasped and shook her head, trying not to let his harshness hurt so much. "I never claimed a future together, Harm."

His dark eyes narrowed. "But you sure as hell put yourself firmly in my *present*." Slicing his hand toward the sofa, he bit out, "Every fucking thing that happened last night was made up bullshit! Why, Jena?"

"I'm sorry, Harm. I was in a panic when you got knocked out and couldn't remember. All I wanted was to—"

"You know what...save your lies for the next idiot," he sneered, then turned and grabbed his hat from the table. Pulling the car and house key from his pocket, he set them on the table, then jammed the Stetson onto his head. His boot heels pounded the wood floor as he strolled past her as if they've never met and walked out the door.

She started to go after him, to try to fully apologize, when the phone started ringing.

Heaving a sigh, Jena answered, "Hello?"

"What the hell is going on, Jena? I just got off the phone with Harm not long ago. Why haven't you agreed to sign the papers?"

She peered through the kitchen window and watched Harm stalk along the drive, his stride steady and determined. "I'm not selling, Ty."

"What? This is ridiculous. When are you going to grow up? You can't just keep flitting through life, doing things at your whim. Other people are involved—"

"I'll sell part of my land to Harm and you can sell him your half, but I want the house, her car, and a couple acres around it. That should be fair to everyone."

A heavy sigh gusts in her ear. "I'd rather not parcel the land up like that. Harm was pretty clear that he wants all of it. Listen, I need to get back to Maryland for meetings on Monday. You said you were going to take a vacation soon. Why don't you stay put and spend some time here before you make such a big decision like moving here permanently. I suspect that by time I'm able to fly back in a few weeks you'll be ready to sell. Texas isn't anything like Maryland, Jena."

I know it's not. It's exactly what I want. "Go on back to Maryland, Ty. Don't worry. I'll be fine here. I'll see you in a few weeks."

Once she hung up, Jena forced thoughts of Harm to the back of her mind. She had a feeling he wasn't up to listening to any apology or explanation she offered and wouldn't be for a while. Looking around the sparse house, she mumbled, "I hope Aunt Sally's car battery isn't dead. I need to get to the store for some supplies."

She'd forgotten how quaint Boone's town center was with its old-style clapboard storefronts and the warm sun shinning on their big picture windows. Jena glanced up at the huge white banner buffeting in the warm breeze over Main Street as it advertised an upcoming festival. She smiled as townsfolk waved as they passed each other on the street. Never saw that living in a big town. A few cars drove past, but for the most part people were out running errands on foot or walking their dogs, or just strolling through the park across the street from the town's center.

A dark-haired woman in her mid-fifties reached the convenience store's door at the same time Jena did. Pulling the door open for her, the woman smiled. "Nice morning."

"That it is," Jena replied, smiling back. "Thanks."

"No problem. You new in town or just visiting?"

Jena inwardly chuckled. That's another thing that would never happen where she lived in Maryland—total strangers asking you personal questions. Grabbing a pushcart while the woman picked up a wire basket from its rack, Jena nodded. "A bit of both actually. I'm staying in my great aunt's place."

"Oh?" The woman's light brown eyes lit up. "Who's your aunt?'"

Jena turned the cart's wheels around. "Sally Tanner."

The woman's expression instantly filled with sympathy as she stepped closer and patted Jena's arm. "I'm so sorry about her passing, dear. Sally was inspiring woman and a great neighbor." Putting her hand out, she said, "I'm Mary O'Don- nell. I live a few miles down the road from Sally's place."

Jena shook her hand. "Jena Hudson. It's nice to meet you."

Releasing Jena's hand Mary tilted her head, her gaze full of questions. "Are you going to live at Sally's place then? I didn't see a For Sale sign on the Double D property, which made me wonder who got the land since she didn't have a family of her own to leave it to."

Jena nodded. "My brother and I inherited the land and her house. I'll be living there now."

"Excellent!" Mary said, rocking on her heels as if she couldn't contain her happiness.

Jena gave a half-laugh. "*I* think so at least. My brother thinks differently. Well, I guess I'd better get the supplies I came for. It was nice meeting you, Mary."

"Pooh on him. You'll love it here. It's nice meeting you too, Jena." As Jena started to back away, Mary continued, "I'll bring you a welcome casserole sometime soon."

Jena paused. "You don't have to do that."

Mary's smile broadened. "It'll be my pleasure. Truly. Take care."

Once Mary headed off, Jena took a deep breath and stared up at the aisle's signs. "May as well start on aisle one."

LATER IN THE afternoon after exploring Sally's property on horseback, Jena had just started to head down the main trail that led back to the house when an Irish Setter streaked across the worn down path, quickly followed by a blond, curly-haired boy calling out, "Quit chasing rabbits, Gimp! Dad'll kill me if I'm late for dinner again this week."

He'd paused for just a second and gave Jena a quick glance before dashing into the woods after his dog. Unfortunately their sudden appearance had startled the horse. As soon as he reared up, Jena let go of the reins in order to quickly grab the saddle horn to keep from falling off.

"Whoa, boy!" she called out forcefully, but he was too worked up. His hooves fell to the ground only to lift up in the air once more, this time accompanied by a panicked whinny.

While she attempted to hold onto the saddle horn with one hand and grab the flying reins with the other, two loud whistles shot through the air and her horse instantly settled.

Jena jerked her gaze to the source of the noise to see Harm sitting on a horse not twenty feet away, his expression thunderous.

Great. Has he come to yell at me some more? Leaning over so she could compose her expression, she retrieved the reins and waited for Harm to walk his horse up to hers.

"What the hell were you thinking going off riding?"

Her spine stiffened as she looked at him. She couldn't see his eyes; the cowboy hat shrouded them in shadows, but the terseness in his voice was enough to set her on edge. "I'm checking out the property. What are you doing here? I figured you'd had enough of me for one day."

Brackets formed around his mouth. He was so cold and distant it's hard to believe this was the same man she met at the hotel the day before.

"I'm here to conduct business, Jena. If you recall, that part of our negotiation never happened."

"I'm not selling," she said as she moved her horse around his and nudged it forward.

"The hell you aren't," he grated out as he pulled up beside her. "We had a deal."

She glanced his way and tried to ignore the pain in her heart. The anger in his eyes really affected her, more than it should. But last night she'd felt so connected to him, like she'd known him for years. How could that evaporate so quickly? Was it really *all* a fantasy? Her heart squeezed at the thought. "You had a deal with my brother. Not with me. He still wants to sell and I'm willing to sell part of my half, but I want the house, the barn, and a couple of acres."

He shook his head in two fast jerks. "I want it all, Jena."

Her spine stiffened. "Too bad. You aren't getting it."

Harm's hand landed on hers, yanking the horse's reins. When her horse halted, he glared at her. "It's bad enough you fucked with my head last night. I won't let you screw with my business too."

Jena jerked her hands from under his and glared back at him. "First of all, there was *two* of us in that bed, Harm, not one. I tried to apologize, but you wouldn't hear me out, so I'm done making an effort on that front. Second, I'm not trying to fuck you over. I sincerely *want* the land and the house. I've made you a fair counter offer. You're just refusing to take it."

His jaw worked as his hard gaze drilled into hers. "Don't go riding alone again."

She curled her fingers tight around the leather reins and counted to five to keep from yelling at him. "I'll go riding any time I damn well please."

"Not on *my* horses, you won't."

Jena glanced down at her mount. The horse *had* instantly responded to his whistles. Meeting his gaze, she shrugged. "I didn't know he was yours. Be sure to take your horses with you when you leave."

"My horses aren't going anywhere. Sally gave me permission to use her stables and they'll stay there until I decide to move them."

"Not in *my* stables, they won't."

"Jena—"

"Give and take, Harm. Give and take." She threw his words back at him, eyebrows raised in challenge.

Harm clamped his mouth shut and turned to stare straight ahead. Nudging his horse forward, he said in a gruff tone, "Let's get back. It'll be dark soon."

Jena followed behind him, a bit of satisfaction warming her heart. Their relationship might've been entirely made up, but if Harm hadn't figured it out already, he'd soon learn that the Jena he met last night was one-hundred-percent real.

6

Jena hadn't seen Harm in a couple weeks. She didn't count the few times she'd seen him shadowing her while she took a horse to explore more of her aunt's property. Harm did come by everyday to take care of the horses, but he always came before she woke. If it weren't for the mucked stalls and freshly replenished food and water in the horses' troughs, she'd never know he was there.

During that time, she'd updated pictures, lamps, and throw pillows, purchased new sheets and a comforter for the bed, then restocked all the household items that had been donated. She'd even put a new flowerbed in the yard, installed big pavers leading down the drive to the barn, and added flower planters on the front porch as well. The house was finally starting to look lived in once more. But during all her home improvement efforts, she grew angrier and angrier that Harm continued to take care of the horses like some kind of spirit in the night—a virile, handsome spirit she never got to see—especially since two of the four horses in the stables were Sally's.

The past four days, she'd gotten up in the wee hours to take care of all four horses herself. As each day passed, she'd had to get up earlier and earlier, because Harm started coming earlier each day too. It'd become a stupid way to avoid and one-up each other, but she didn't care. What she did care about was the faulty light fixture in the rafters that kept flickering in and out. It made working in the early morning hours difficult. On the fifth day, the job was taking longer than normal, because the light stayed off longer and longer. She'd only made it three-fourths of the way through mucking when the bulb flashed bright then went completely out.

Burnt out. Crap. Once she retrieved a new light bulb from the storage box, Jena tucked it in her overalls front pocket and moved over to the wall to retrieve the shorter ladder from its hooks. An extra tall ladder had been hooked above it, but it was awkward to get down at this height. Setting the ladder against one of the beams, she managed to climb to the rafter and crawl across it until she reached the light in the center of the barn.

Since the light bulb was underneath the rafter, replacing it from above took some finesse. Dangling her legs on either side of the beam, Jena used the thick rounded bolt jutting out from the side of the beam to support herself as she leaned over to unscrew the dead bulb, then tossed it below. Screwing the new bulb in turned into a different challenge. She couldn't quite get the right angle to seat it properly in the socket. Hooking her thigh around the beam for support, she edged over slightly and rested her belly against the bolt until she could finally settle the bulb in the socket. As it glowed bright with the final turn, she smiled, but her triumph quickly faded as her anchoring leg slipped and she went over the edge of the rafter.

Heart juddering, she fell so fast Jena didn't have time to grab onto the beam. Just as her leg cleared the rafter, she was quickly jerked to a stop. One of the belt loops on her overalls had caught on the bolt she'd been leaning against for leverage, hanging her like a piñata twelve feet above the floor.

Jena tried to free herself, but her own weight and the odd angle she hung made unhooking herself impossible. Then again, she glanced at the ground below and grimaced. If she did manage to free herself, her hands could slip as she attempted to climb her way back around to the top of the rafter. She didn't want to find out what a fall from this height felt like.

"How did you even *manage* that?"

Harm's voice coming from directly underneath her made her cringe. Why'd he have to decide to show up late today? She chanced a quick glance his way, moving as little as possible. How long would the belt loop hold? Harm stood looking up at her with the dead light bulb in his hand. "Can you just help me out here, please?"

She heard the big ladder being lifted and felt the metal land against the rafter a few feet away from her head. A few seconds later, Harm sat on the rafter, his legs dangling down the other side as he peered at her belt loop, scowling. Turning hard eyes her way, he grated, "You could've broken your damned neck."

"Think how much easier your life would be if I had." She let the sarcasm flow, because she hated how attractive he looked in a chambray button down shirt, the edges of his hair, still damp from his shower, peeking from underneath his Stetson. Even upside down and staring at her with a disapproving frown, he was sexy as hell. She refused to inhale his clean, masculine scent. Why torture herself?

"Seriously, Jena." His tone settled to an even one. "What were you thinking?"

"Just shut up and free me already."

Harm pressed his mouth together, then leaned over her. "As you wish." With the flick of his wrist, he popped the straining threads on her belt loop.

Jena screamed all the way down. She landed on her back in the thick pile of hay she'd mucked from the stalls but had yet to move. As the foul smell of manure and urine quickly seeped through the overalls' denim, it took her a few seconds to process the shock slamming through her.

Ignoring Harm's outstretched hand to help her up, she pushed herself to her feet from the pile of stench-filled hay. "That was just shitty!" she hissed through clenched teeth. "There was a million other ways you could've helped me down."

While she shuddered, then swiped off the shit and piss-soaked hay caking her backside from head to toe, Harm didn't bother to hide his amusement; his dark eyes sparked with mirth. "You told me to free you already, so I did. I knew you wouldn't get hurt."

Jena's chest heaved with pent up fury, but instead of yelling at him, she decided she'd get her own revenge. Pulling the rubber band from her ponytail, she shook the sticky bits of hay from her hair, then unhooked the straps of the overalls. Stepping out of the wet, soiled material and her boots, she stood in front of Harm wearing nothing but a white tank top and underwear.

When Harm's gaze lowered to her nipples clearly showing through the thin white shirt, she inwardly reveled at the flash of heat flaring in their chocolate brown depths. Keeping her face perfectly composed, she stripped out of her tank and the tiny scrap of underwear then dropped them on the pile of stinky clothes.

"Jena..." Harm said in a low tone, amusement completely gone as he took a step closer. Just as his gaze returned to her face, she turned and walked out of the barn with her chin held high.

As she opened the front door, Harm's reflection in the glass made her pause for a split second; he stood in the doorway of the barn watching her, his hands fisted by his sides. But thoughts of how she'd laid in bed every single night since their passionate time together, reliving memories and desperately wanting him all over again rushed forth. She stiffened her spine and smirked as she walked inside.

An hour later, Jena was surprised to see Harm shutting a stall door when she strolled into the barn. A long shower had cooled her simmering frustration while bolstering her determination to finish the job she'd left behind. The muck pile and the clothes she'd planned to trash had disappeared. Only her boots sat by the barn door. Once again, the horses had been fed and watered. "Why'd you do that?" she said, gesturing to the empty space where the pile had been.

Harm shrugged. "It needed to be done."

"I was coming back to finish up, Harm. Maybe if you take your horses, I won't feel obligated to take care of them."

"I told you I'm not moving them until the deal is done."

Jena spread her hands wide. "And I'm not selling all the land. So who's going to camp out and make the earliest shift tomorrow, hmm?"

Harm's mouth tightened as the tension between them rose. "I can take care of—"

"Hello?" a man's voice cut Harm off.

Jena turned to the dark-haired cowboy wearing faded jeans, scuffed boots, and a lopsided smile on his face. He stood in the doorway of the barn holding a casserole dish, his eyebrows raised. She returned his smile as she approached. "Hi."

"Are you Jena Hudson?"

She nodded. "The one and only."

His smile shifted to a full grin. "I'm Hunter, Mary's son." Holding the dish toward her, he continued, "My mom asked me to bring this casserole by."

"That was so nice of her," she said, taking the dish. "Please tell your mom I said, 'thank you for thinking of me.'"

He nodded and touched the brim of his straw cowboy hat. "Will do. My mom also asked me to ask you if you'd like to volunteer for a charity event she's running at the summer festival on Saturday. It's a dance-a-thon type thing. You shouldn't have to work the whole time. There'll be games and rides and great food. She said it'd be a good way for you to meet lots of people from Boone."

"That sounds great. Hopefully I'll meet some people in the medical community. I'm a nurse and will be looking for a job soon."

Hunter pushed his hands into his jean pockets. "I'm sure my mom can introduce you to the hospital administrator."

"That would be great." Jena pressed the warm casserole

dish to her belly, wrapping her arms around it. "What's the charity event about?"

"It's for juvenile diabetes. We lost my youngest brother to it, so Mom's a big supporter."

Jena's smile faltered slightly. "Oh, I'm sorry to hear that. Yes, please tell your mom I'd be happy to help in any way I can."

Hunter's green eyes lit up. "Great! I'll pick you up around seven-thirty and drive you over."

"See you then."

Glancing up at Harm, who casually leaned against the stall door he'd just closed, Hunter said, "Hey Harm." When Harm only grunted in response, he shrugged and returned his attention to her. "Guess I'd better get going. See you on Saturday." Grinning as he backed away, a devilish light reflected in his eyes. "Promise you'll save me a dance?"

Jena laughed and nodded.

Once he headed back down the driveway where he'd left his truck idling, Harm's voice came from directly behind her. "Keep your guard up. That one's got more hands than heart."

It took everything she had not to snap her gaze to his and snort. As she walked off to put the casserole dish away, Jena said over her shoulder, "Thanks for the advice, Tin Man. I'll be fine."

LATER IN THE AFTERNOON, the sound of something metal clanking against the hard ground woke Jena from a much needed nap. She'd spent four exhausting hours in the hot sun scraping and sanding down the peeling paint from the porch railing and spindles in preparation to repaint. At some point she'd tackle the outside shutters too; they looked just as sun-faded and worn.

Peering through her curtains, she saw a man in his late fifties standing beside the fence patting one of Harm's horses on the neck. When he moved to lift a bridle toward the horse, she quickly jumped up and slipped her feet inside her tennis shoes. By the time she got them laced, the man had started leading the first horse up the metal ramp into the transport trailer hooked to the back of his truck.

Jena rushed outside, almost tripping over a wrapped up package leaning against her front door as she called out, "Excuse me! What are you doing?"

While she used her foot to slide the dry cleaners' clear plastic bundle of jean overalls and white underclothes out of the way, the older man paused and pushed his cowboy hat back.

Surprise flickered across his tanned, leathery features as he watched her approach. "Evenin' Miss...?" He trailed off and raised his eyebrows.

"Jena Hudson," she supplied quickly. "And you are?"

"Name's Jack." He squinted against the late afternoon sun. "You own Sally's place now?"

She nodded. "Sally was my Great Aunt."

One corner of his mouth crooked. "Sally was a good woman. She sure could cook."

"I remember her wonderful meals." Jena nodded her agreement and tucked her fingers in her front pockets. "You're Harm's foreman?"

"Yep." He patted the horse's neck. "Finally getting around to bringing these horses over to Steele Way."

Jena's heart jerked. "Harm's moving them?"

The man tugged on his ear. "Harm's been spending so much time over here lately. Getting up earlier and earlier has made him a hundred kinds of asinine." He flicked his tongue across his teeth, his assessing gaze holding hers. "Yep, the animals seemed to be distracting him."

"Oh, I see." Jena bit her bottom lip and tried not to let her disappointment show. Her chest ached at the idea she wouldn't catch any more glimpses of Harm now that he wouldn't have a reason to stop by every day. Sparring with Harm was better than no Harm. At least then she could imagine that deep down he felt something for her beyond intense dislike. And that she hadn't totally made up the amazing chemistry between them. Harm had her soiled clothes laundered. That had to count for something, right? Then again, those close to him apparently didn't think his time here was in his best interest. Sighing, she gestured to the barn. "His other horse is in there."

The older man eyed her for a couple of seconds, then snorted and turned Harm's horse around. As he led the animal down the ramp and back toward the fence, Jena followed, completely baffled by his contradictory action. She watched in silence as he took off the bridle and swatted the horse's rump to encourage him to roam once more.

Jack didn't say a word; he just closed the gate, then headed for his truck. Jena quickly caught up to his shuffling stride. "Wait...I'm confused. I thought you were taking the horses?"

He climbed inside the truck, its heavy metal door creaking as he shut it. Leaning out the open window, he nodded and tugged on the rim of his hat. "Sometimes we need a little distraction."

Jena grinned. She liked this "real" Jack even better than her made up version. "Your boss is a very stubborn man."

He let out a hearty laugh. "That he is, ma'am." Patting the truck's door, he started the engine, then called out as he drove off, "Nice meeting ya."

7

The next morning, Jena got up at sunrise. Harm hadn't come and gone yet, so she took care of the horses. The morning was a cool one, overcast with just a slight nip in the air. She knew it wouldn't last; the Texas sun would soon burn off the coolness, so she saddled a horse and took advantage of the nice morning, heading down her drive to take a path alongside the main road.

After a couple hours of exploring side roads, it started to drizzle. Jena made her way back to the main road. *So much for painting today.* Just as she turned down the road that led to her drive, she had to quickly jerk her horse onto the low embankment. An old truck zoomed past at breakneck speed, wet dirt splattering behind its wheels and up onto the plastic-covered big screen TV anchored down in the truck bed.

Yelling after the reckless driver, she eased the horse back onto the road. The drizzle turned to light rain as she continued toward her drive.

She paused for a second when she saw Harm's truck

parked beside the barn. Didn't he notice she'd done the chores already? Had he discovered his foreman came by yesterday? She had a feeling Jack wouldn't volunteer that information, so why was he still here? Curious, she nudged her horse into a faster pace, trotting the rest of the way up the drive.

Once she didn't find Harm in the barn, she glanced toward the house, wondering if he was inside, but her gaze caught on his boot print impressions in the damp ground leading away from the barn.

Jena quickly tied the horse's reins on a post inside the barn, then grabbed an umbrella from her car. Before the rain washed away Harm's path, she followed it.

The rain started coming down harder just as she spied Harm a few feet in the woods off a side road. He was lowering something with red hair into a shallow hole he'd dug in the ground. Emotion welled when she realized it was the Irish Setter she'd seen that boy chasing not that long ago. Had he accidentally hit the poor dog?

She watched in silence as Harm used the shovel she'd seen hanging on the wall in her barn to shovel the dirt back onto the makeshift grave.

When he was almost done, he glanced up and caught her gaze. Anger, not regret, filled his expression before he returned to his task.

Harm had just finished covering the grave as the sound of the boy calling, "Gimp, where are you boy? We have to head back. Gimp!" echoed around them. The voice resonated from the same direction Jena had come, sounding agitated, and the boy was getting closer.

As Harm stepped onto the road next to her, Jena lowered

the umbrella behind her to block the view of the shovel laying on the disturbed ground just as the kid came around the bend.

The boy paused for a second, his eyes wide with surprise at seeing them on the road, but then he quickly approached. "Have you seen Gimp running around, Harm?"

The rain made a dull thudding sound on the brim of Harm's hat as he shook his head and slid his dirt-covered fingers into his back pockets. "Sorry, Jacob. Haven't seen Gimp today."

Frustration flickered in the boy's eyes. "I've got to get him. I'm supposed to already be home. We've got errands to run. Dad'll be ticked that I made him late."

Thunder rumbled and Harm looked up right as lightning streaked across the darkening sky. Returned his gaze to the boy, he said, "You should head back home. It's not safe to be in the woods with lighting going on."

"But Gimp—"

"He knows the way home. Now go on," Harm countered in a gruff voice.

Jacob started to turn away, then glanced at the open umbrella Jena held. "Don't look like it's doin' ya much good like that."

Jena shrugged and offered a wry smile. "I'm already wet at this point."

Shaking his head at her, the boy took off running back up the road.

Once Jacob was out of sight, Jena pulled the umbrella back over her head and started back toward the barn.

She'd just removed the saddle and pad, then picked up a towel to dry the wet horse when the barn door creaked with

Harm's entrance. She heard him hook the shovel back on the wall, but didn't turn away from her task of rubbing the wet horse down.

Thunder rumbled and the rain beat down on the barn's roof. Its fierce wind buffeting against the barn's heavy door reminded her of that night together with Harm. She took a deep breath and shook off the memories, rubbing along the horse's back in fast circles.

Harm's solid frame spread across her back as his hand landed on hers. Even through their wet clothes she could feel his warmth. "I didn't hit his dog, Jena."

She stilled herself and tried not to let his hard frame hovering close affect her. "It was probably that truck with the TV in the back. The driver was crazy. He almost ran into me on the road a half hour ago."

Harm's hand tensed over hers for a second. Releasing her, he didn't step back as he answered in a terse tone. "That was Jacob's father."

Jena stepped away and faced him, shocked. "Are you serious?"

Harm's jaw muscle jumped and anger flared anew in his gaze. "I heard him in town yesterday at the store ranting about his family dragging him down. Claimed he was going to just up and leave them first chance he got. I was on my way to your place when I saw him hit the dog."

Jena blinked, her heart aching for Jacob. "So the boy just lost his father too?"

Harm's mouth twisted, his eyes darkening in intense dislike. "Believe me, they're better off. Molly's strong. She'll prosper without that leech around."

She tilted her head and considered him for a second. "You just lied to that boy's face."

Harm stiffened. "Hell yeah, I lied. He doesn't need to know his father mowed his dog down like a weed he couldn't wait to eradicate on his way out of town. There's no reason to break the kid's heart."

Sure she understood why, but how could Harm not see the irony. She couldn't help but raise her eyebrow.

"What?" Harm asked, but when she just stared at him, his face hardened and his gaze narrowed. "Don't even try to tell me you lied because you didn't want to break my heart. A guy you *just* met."

Actually, yeah it had been for his benefit—at least partially—but Harm wouldn't believe her. Jena shook her head and turned back to drying the horse. It'd been for her benefit too, so why not tell him that part at least. "No, I was trying not to break mine. You made it clear you didn't believe in happy-ever-afters. And I think there's someone out there for everyone. I wanted to believe you were the kind of guy who *could* believe. That you were capable." Glancing over her shoulder, she sighed at his stony expression and continued, "Yes, I was wrong to lie to you. I deeply apologize for that." Turning back to the horse, she ran the towel from his neck all the way to his rump. "But I won't apologize for holding onto my beliefs, no matter how naïve they seem to you. Now if you'll excuse me, I've got to get this work done so I can drive into town. I have some errands to run."

Without another word, Harm turned and walked out of the barn.

JENA HADN'T SPOKEN to Harm in a couple of days—not anything of consequence at least. The last two mornings, he'd arrived right around sunrise—her preferred time to take care of the horses—and they worked on their respective animals until the job was done. If Harm needed one of the grooming brushes or the tool to clean pebbles from his horse's hooves, he asked and she handed it over, or visa versa. She assumed that was as close to a compromise as she was going to get from him on the horse issue, but his quietness was getting to her.

On one hand, it felt like they'd turned a corner, but on the other, she was beginning to believe they'd taken twenty steps back. The more she thought about it, the more Harm's calm politeness was grating on her last nerve. Here they were, halfway through their second day of civility—acting like strangers working on their horses side by side at a boarding stable—and she was pretty sure she had fresh grind marks on her back teeth.

Blowing her hair out of her face, she chanced a glance at Harm as he bent to brush Ranger's chest and belly one last time. Wearing a dark green t-shirt, Harm's corded forearm muscles flexed with his movements, while his faded Wranglers' soft denim cupped his butt like they were made just for him.

She shook her head to clear the wayward thoughts that instantly took her back to their night together, then lifted her gaze to his profile. He hadn't shaved this morning and the stubble on his face, a few shades darker than his hair, only made him look more irresistibly rugged. How could one man look so good? Harm seemed completely oblivious to her appreciative perusal; he stayed focused on his task, his face perfectly impassive as he worked. *What was going on in his head?*

Finally, she couldn't take it any more. She didn't care if she pissed him off, but she wanted to know why he was being so even-tempered. Was he working some new kill-her-with-politeness angle in the hopes he'd get her to sell? This Harm was a far cry from their earlier interactions, and she wasn't at all sure she liked or trusted him. Clearing her throat, she opened her mouth to speak when his phone rang.

"Hey Jack. Yeah, I'm interested in buying a couple more stallions. I know space is getting slim, so only two for now. Can Hank come by in an hour? All right. Be there in a few."

As Harm ended the call, Jena exited her stall and walked into his horse's stall. Holding out her hand for the brush, she said, "Go. I'll take care of the rest."

His brows pulled together. "Are you sure? I can come back later."

She sighed. "Of course. Take care of whatever business you need to."

"Thanks, Jena."

As Harm set the brush in her hand, the barest contact of his fingers brushing her palm sent tingles jumping along her arm. Jena dropped her gaze as the goose bumps that quickly followed raised the tiny hairs on her skin.

Her breath caught when Harm released the brush to trace his finger along the side of her arm, pressing the raised hairs back into place. She'd never been so deeply affected by another man. Her emotions for him hadn't changed one bit since that night—well, so long as she ignored the frustrated parts. Just as her gaze lifted to his, his phone rang again, breaking the tenuous, electric moment between them.

Harm turned away to pat his horse's neck while he spoke into his phone in a low voice. "I'm coming, Jack. What? Okay, I'll bring Ranger."

Hanging up, he glanced over his shoulder and offered a wry smile. "Looks like you won't need to finish up after all. Jack wants to show off Ranger. I'm convinced the man thinks the horses are his kids."

Jena swallowed the sudden lump in her throat. Harm acted as if he'd never touched her. Had she imagined the intimate moment? Maybe he'd been brushing dirt off her arm and meant nothing else by it. Forcing an unaffected smile, she nodded and backed out of the stall. "I'll leave you to it then."

Harm held her gaze for a second. "When is your brother coming into town again? He mentioned he'd be back last time I talked to him."

Was he hoping to get her brother to convince her to sell? He had been talking about a lack of space for his horses. Everything inside her seized up. He may as well have thrown a cup of cold water in her face. New angle, same goal. Damn, she hated being right. "He'll be here next week." Tilting her head, she continued, "You really can't operate on middle ground, can you?"

He frowned. "No. The house—"

"Won't be included in the deal," she cut him off. "I told you I'd sell you a portion of the land, Harm. You'll get the space you need for your horses," she managed to finish in an even tone even though she shook with anger inside.

He opened his mouth to say something, then shook his

head before turning to retrieve Ranger's saddle and pad from the saddle rack.

THE ENTIRE TIME he'd been working alongside Jena the last couple of days, all Harm could think about was how good she'd smelled and felt in his arms that night they'd spent together. That one night of utter bullshit! The past few weeks had been easier to wallow in his anger, to roll around in its thick protection and coat himself good so Jena wouldn't wiggle her way inside his head once again. Keeping her squarely pegged as the conniving, self-serving woman who'd used him as her own personal entertainment toy, a woman whose lies he'd been fool enough to buy into like a blinded idiot, had mostly worked to dampen his attraction for her.

Until yesterday.

What she'd said about her reasons for lying—that she wanted to believe he was capable of believing in a happy-ever-after—pretty much jerked the rug of indignant righteousness out from under his boots. She'd even called him Tin Man. Did she really believe he didn't have a heart? Or was she just messing with his head yet again, pulling her wily feminine strings and pushing his buttons to convince him he was totally at fault in how everything between them turned out? Damn the woman twisted him up; he wasn't sure what he felt anymore.

He didn't quite know what to make of Jena. Her brother said she was a free spirit, but even though his head tried to remind him she'd been deceitful and manipulative, his heart didn't want to believe her intentions were so calculating. He'd stayed quiet the past couple of days mainly because he didn't trust himself around her. He didn't trust that he wouldn't start to believe in some parts of the story she'd woven about them. He wasn't going to be stupid enough to make a fool out of himself all over again

He knew asking about her brother would make her angry. It had been for an entirely different reason, but he let her believe what she wanted. It was a low-down thing to do, but being around her made it easier and easier to forget that night wasn't real. All those thoughts chipped away at his resolve to keep his distance, which in turn raised his self-preservation hackles to full defense mode.

For both their sakes, he had to keep his wits firmly intact. The last thing he needed was to go down that path twice. She made it clear she believed in a white knight carrying her off into the sunset. Sadly, she was right about one thing; he wasn't capable of that kind of grand gesture or the crazy leap of faith that came with it. Yep, it was best for him to stay the course. He wasn't sure he'd come out sane the next time around.

THE REST of the day flew by as Jena took her frustration with Harm out on the outside shutters. She could've painted the porch instead, but she felt like punching something, so a scraper sloughing away weathered paint was as close as she was going to get. She got so into her project, she skipped lunch and tuned everything out until a male voice called up to her, "You going to the fair like that?"

Jena gasped and dropped the scraper. Holding her hand on her chest, she said, "Geeze, you scared me, Hunter." As his words sank in, she quickly glanced at her watch. "Am I late?"

Dressed in boots, jeans, a big belt buckle shaped like Texas, and a short-sleeved button down shirt, he thumbed his hat back, then bent to retrieve the scraper. As he handed the tool to her, his gaze appreciatively slid up her bare legs. "No, but while I think you look hot as hell up on that ladder in a pair of cut-off shorts and a tank top, you uh...might want to change for the charity event. We need to be there in thirty minutes."

Laughing, Jena hopped down from the ladder. "I think I can meet your deadline."

8

_____

The streets leading to the town center had been blocked off for the festivities. Food vendors lined one side of the main street and carnival vendors running games and fun rides had set up on the other. Jena had never seen so many people at once. She had no idea Boone had grown so much.

Hunter cupped her elbow and guided her through the crowd, past people and strollers. As they dodged around kids clutching ice cream cones or cotton candy in their hands, their eyes wide in wonderment at the pony rides and games with bells and lights flashing, Jena couldn't help but wonder if Harm attended things like this.

If he didn't, she'd totally drag him to the next one just to see him finally loosen up and have some fun. The fact Harm took up so much space in her head, when he was obviously ready to boot her completely from his life dampened her mood a little.

Jena lifted her chin and inhaled deeply, absorbing the smells of salty buttered popcorn mixed with the sweetness of powdered funnel cakes. The scents conjured fond memories of coming here with Ty and her great aunt, chasing thoughts of Harm to the back of her mind.

It also made her realize she hadn't eaten anything other than a bowl of oatmeal this morning. Since they were moving at a brisk pace to make it to the event on time, now wouldn't be the best time to stop and buy a hotdog. Hunter had promised her she wouldn't have to work the whole night, so she ignored her growling belly and let him lead her to his mother's event.

"Jena's here," Hunter called to his mom who was talking to a DJ setting up his equipment just inside the entrance of a huge twenty-five foot by twenty-five foot cordoned off area. Tiny Christmas lights hung in crisscross fashion over the entire squared-off space, giving off a soft warm glow against the dusky sky.

Mary glanced up and waved, saying, "Be there in a sec." While she finished up her conversation with the DJ,

A long line was just starting to form in front of the booth just outside the cordoned entrance. On the other side of the line, a crowd of guys huddled around a bulletin board sporting the bold red title: **Tenth Annual Juvenile Diabetes Charity Event. Select Your Dance Partner(s). With only fifty slots, their cards fill up fast, so don't wait!**

Jena's gaze strayed to the girl selling tickets. That job didn't look too taxing. Hopefully she'd only have to work the ticket booth for an hour.

As the crowd of guys standing in front of the bulletin board made their way over to the back of the long line to buy tickets, a few of them glanced her way and smiled. Friendly bunch. She smiled back and was surprised when a couple of them pulled out their wallets and pointed to her. *What was that about?*

Then several more guys in line cast their gazes her way and did a double-take. The line moved up, but the men kept staring at her instead of moving. The break in the line finally allowed her a view of the contents on the bulletin board. Her jaw dropped when she stared back at a picture of herself in a lineup of potential dance partners for the charity event. She and nine other women in their mid-twenties were being auctioned off. Well, at least her dance time was. People could buy a dance with her that lasted one song.

Her gaze widened in disbelief as she looked at Mary leaning over the DJ and pointing to something in his three-ring binder. A list of songs maybe? Mary must've snapped that picture of her while she was shopping a week ago. Thank goodness she'd put on makeup and curled her hair that day she'd bumped into Mary at the supermarket. The three times Jena had seen Mary around town, the woman's bob haircut was tucked behind her ears, and she had on casual shorts and a cotton top. Today, Mary's hair was coiffed to beauty-salon-meets-a-can-of-hairspray perfection, and she rocked a vibrant coral blouse under a sharp navy blazer she'd buttoned over matching slacks. Mary had transformed her look so completely for this event, Jena couldn't help but feel a little duped. She swung her gaze to Hunter. "Why didn't you tell me I was *part* of the main attraction?"

He looked completely taken aback. "I told you it was a dance-a-thon."

She pursed her lips. "That didn't convey at all."

"You dance, right?"

She nodded. "Of course, but—"

"It's for charity, Jena." He smiled and shrugged. "Then, no biggie."

That's easy for you to say.

"I'm planning to buy a couple dances myself," he said, winking at her. "In the end, the kids benefit. That's all that matters."

What could she say to that? Dang, right now she felt a kinship with the horses Harm planned to buy from that guy— did she have nice teeth, sleek lines, and good hindquarters? Was she a smooth, pleasurable ride? But unlike the horses getting Harm's undivided attention, here she stood, being auctioned off for the bargain price of...

Jena squinted at the board to see the cost per dance. Twenty bucks! For a three-to-four minute song? She barely resisted the urge to whistle. At those rates, and if every girl's card filled up, Mary would raise *good* money for her charity over the course of the two-and-a-half hour event. This woman definitely had some business savvy.

Jena chanced a glance at the line of men waiting to buy tickets; a couple of them openly leered at her, and one pointed to her, then formed a heart with his hands over his chest. Then again, four minutes might seem like an eternity. Suddenly she regretted wearing a blue jersey dress that clung to her curves.

She'd chosen to wear it because Harm made her feel like she blended right into the barn walls. The electric color definitely made her stand out, so she thought a little attention would do her ego some good, but now her stomach clenched at just how much attention she seemed to be drawing. Her belly's sudden rumbling growl didn't help settle her nerves; now she felt nauseous too. Ugh, she really regretted not grabbing that hotdog. Swallowing her grimace, Jena focused on the goal of Mary's event. *It's for the kids*, she chanted in her head over and over.

By the time the event was about to start, the sky had darkened and small café tables and chairs had been set up outside the cordoned off dance floor. Many of the chairs were already filled with men waiting for the dance to start. Other people sat in the chairs enjoying the popular pre-event dance music the DJ had been playing for the last twenty minutes.

Clapping her hands, Mary picked up the mic and beckoned Jena and the ladies standing outside the dance floor. "Come on in, ladies. Line up over there, single file so everyone can see you."

Once they'd done as she asked, Mary swept her hand toward them as she spoke to the crowd. "Give these ladies a big round of applause, won't ya?"

Everyone began to clap, and many of the guys whistled while a few hooted and hollered.

Mary beamed. "All right. Settle down. Are you all ready for the Tenth Annual Juvenile Diabetes Dance to start?"

"Hell yeah. Get on with it, Marybeth!" an older man in a flannel shirt, dark jeans, and black boots called out.

She gave him a stern look. "Watch your manners, Sam, especially on the dance floor." Turning her gaze back to the crowd, she continued, "That goes for all of you who buy dances tonight. There will be no inappropriate groping of the wonderful ladies who've volunteered their time to help out. If I so much as catch you tryin' it, you'll be booted—with no refund—and someone else can buy your slot. Got it?"

A round of masculine agreements rumbled through the crowd.

Nodding, Mary turned to address the line-up of women as she pulled a stack of index-sized cards out of her blazer pocket. "Okay, ladies. I have your cards here." A pleased smile lit up her face as she flipped through them, then glanced up at the crowd. "Some cards are filled. There are about twenty slots left. We've got a listing of who still has some availability over at the sign-up booth." She flashed a mega-watt smile. "And don't forget...each card can have one more slot added if you're willing to pay the premium price for it."

While Mary reminded everyone of the options and rules of the event, Jena whispered to the redhead next to her, "What's the going rate for premium price?"

The girl smiled as she brushed her long, wavy hair over her shoulder. "Fifty. My card's full, plus the premium dance."

Jena slid her gaze down to the girl's very generous rack pushing against her black v-neck dress. "I take it you've done this before?"

She nodded. "Three years running. This year my card filled in five minutes. That's a new record. Last year was fifteen." Her gaze flicked to a bear of a guy standing just outside the dance area; his arms crossed over his barrel chest and a deep scowl creased his brow. "My boyfriend's livid he couldn't afford to buy the whole card, but I committed to this before I met him, so..."

Jena put her hand over her stomach to muffle the rumbling. Her nerves really didn't help matters. "Someone can buy a whole card?"

"If they can afford the upcharge. Sure."

"What's the upcharge?"

The redhead giggled. "Twenty-five per dance."

Jena quickly did the math. Twelve hundred and fifty dollars! Mary's running quite the racket. "That's crazy expensive."

"Yes it is. I'm Sophie, by the way."

"I'm Jena." Jena swept her gaze back to the crowd as the men who bought the first dance started to line up just outside the entrance. Hunter was standing at the ticket booth with this wallet in hand. "Guess I'm as ready for this as I'll ever be."

Mary walked down the line of girls, handing them their cards. Since she was the last one in line, Jena shifted from one foot to the other while Mary spoke to each of the girls. God, what if she only had a couple of slots filled? Those men might've liked the way she looked, but the cost wasn't cheap. Then again, Hunter was over there buying a couple of dances, so she wouldn't look like a total reject.

Mary shook her head and chuckled as she handed Jena hers. "I thought Sophie would be the one this year, but you've just broken another record."

Jena takes the card, and when she sees a big red X has been stamped across it, heat suffused her face. "Um, I don't understand. Does this mean no one bought any dances?" It was on the tip of her tongue to say that Hunter planned to when Mary laughed and patted her on the shoulder.

"No, dear. It means—"

"I bought your card," Harm finished for Mary as he stepped around the older woman and held out his hand. "Care to dance, Miss Hudson?"

Jena's mouth suddenly dried up as she stared at Harm.

He wasn't dressed up like the other guys, who'd come to the event with their hair all combed and wearing their darkest jeans and shiny boots. Harm looked like he did everyday, hair slightly windblown and dressed in scuffed boots, faded denim, and a button down shirt with rolled up sleeves. The only difference was, he wasn't wearing his cowboy hat.

His eyebrow elevated slightly and an amused smile lifted the corner of his lip. "The music has started Jena," he said softly.

He might not be dressed up, but he'd never looked better to her. Jena's hand shook as she set it in his hand and let him lead her to the dance floor. Question after question pinged in her head. *Why did he buy my card? That's a crap-ton of money. Why would he do that? He's pissed at me. God knows he doesn't trust me. It just doesn't make any sense.*

Harm used his hold on her hand to spin her into place in front of him. When his other hand lightly rested at the base of her spine and he began to dance to the slow song, Jena looked up at him. "Why did you do this? This doesn't seem like your kind of thing?"

He stiffened slightly. "I can dance."

She shook her head. "That's not what I meant. This just didn't seem like something you'd be interested in."

He chuckled, then glanced back toward the crowd. "Half the crew from my ranch is here, but yeah this isn't my thing."

Jena saw a few men pointing at them and nodding their approval. "Then why in the world would you torture yourself like this?"

Harm shrugged, his gaze drifting down to hers. "I came into town to run an errand. When I saw the signs Mary had posted about the dance event and you were one of the dance partners, I knew this wasn't what you thought you were signing up for, so I stuck around."

Jena tensed in his arms. "Why didn't you just wait to see if my card filled up? I don't need your pity, Harm."

His fingers flexed on her back. "You think this is me pitying you? Hell no, I figured you didn't want to be groped by total strangers for a few hours." He paused, suddenly going still. "Or was I wrong about that?"

Jena shook her head and squeezed his hand holding hers. "No, I didn't want that, but well..." She shrugged. "It's for charity at least."

Harm resumed dancing, mumbling, "That doesn't make it okay. Mary should've explained what volunteering entailed."

Jena snickered. "Why would she? She just got the biggest donation ever, thanks to you."

Harm snorted. "Don't remind me."

At that moment, Mary tapped Jena on the shoulder. "Just wanted you to know you've got a premium add-on. Hunter bought your last dance."

"Sounds like your charity will do well tonight," Jena said, smiling.

Mary rocked on her heels, her eyes glistening as she glanced at Harm. "Thanks to Mr. Harmon Steele's donation."

Once Mary walked off, and as Harm began to dance once more, guilt wedged in Jena's stomach. She pressed her hand to his back to get him to look at her. "Thank you for the gesture, but I'll give you half the money. You really didn't need to do that."

His dark eyes flashed. "Don't insult me, Jena. I might not have Prince Charming's manners, but I know how to do what's right."

Jena's gaze widened. "I wasn't trying to insult you. I know you're a good man. I—" she paused and bit her lip, unsure what else to say that wouldn't tick him off more. She seemed to have a knack for it.

"Hey." Harm's fingers folded around hers, drawing her gaze back to his. "Truce for tonight?"

Sincerity reflected in his dark brown eyes, and she smiled, nodding.

"Good. 'Cause the last thing I need is for the guys from the ranch to see us fighting. They'll never let me hear the end of it."

Jena wanted to jab him in the gut. What did he mean by *that*? Instead, she forced a smile. "I can pretend if you can."

As the song segued from a slow tune from the fifties to a recent song with a soulful beat, Mary announced, "Okay, time for the next partner." While dancers switched out all around them, Harm and Jena kept their gazes trained on each other.

The amusement in his eyes faded, and a flash of something she couldn't decipher replaced it. "That's one thing you and I do very, very well together."

Not an ounce of blame showed in his eyes, and his voice had dropped to an even deeper bass, hitting Jena straight in the belly. Her heart ramped up several beats and when she realized his gaze had lowered to her mouth, she worked hard not to lick her lips.

Were they pretending now?

She really had no clue, but if tonight was the only time Harm would ever touch her again, she'd damn well enjoy it. Might as well make a memory to hold onto.

Sliding two fingers under his belt loop, she hooked her

thumb along the top of his jeans. "Show me what you've got, Mr. Steele. I'm always willing to learn new moves."

Harm's hand flattened on her lower back. It's warmth seeped into her dress as he slid his palm upward and pulled her a bit closer. "Are you sure you're up for it, Miss Hudson?"

She slipped her hand free of his, then curled it around his neck. Tugging him down as they twirled in a slow circle, she whispered in his ear, "I can take whatever you dish out. Just be prepared to get it back. As you know, I'm *all* about mutual sharing."

When she released him and moved to step out of his personal space, Harm's fingers flexed on her back, his arm around her like a band of steel. "Where do you think you're going?"

"I was giving you your space back."

"What if I *want* you in my space?"

She smiled and flattened her palm on his chest. "Then all you have to do is ask. It's as simple as that."

His eyes shuttered as his expression turned serious. "It's never that simple."

Jena didn't know how to respond to that, but Harm didn't give her a chance to either. He wrapped his arm around her waist and twirled her to the uplifting part in the song.

She realized they were done talking—flirting—whatever they had been doing, but Harm didn't stop dancing.

For the next hour and a half, Jena forgot about being hungry. She forgot about the way they'd originally met or how they'd parted the next day as they danced to various types of music from jazz to pop to country. It surprised her that Harm knew so many different types of dances until he told her his mother taught him when he was a boy. He even taught Jena the two-step, which she found harder than she thought it would be, but she eventually caught on.

When the music finally switched back to a slow song, Harm didn't hesitate. He instantly pulled her body flush with his as if they'd done so a million times before. Jena stiffened for a second, until he whispered in her ear, "Relax. Give a little."

His hips began to move to the sensual song, his movements directing her to follow the rhythm with him. The sensation of his hard chest touching hers, combined with hearing the similar phrasing he'd said to her the first time they had sex, made her pulse race and her insides shake.

Jena tried to keep her thoughts lighthearted and her emotions firmly detached, but Harm's warm hand caressing her lower back, then sliding to her hip to lock her lower body even more firmly to his, made her want him so much she found it hard to breathe.

When this dance event was over, she knew in her heart that Harm would walk away and pretend it had never happened. This was her punishment. The thought made her chest constrict and her head feel woozy. Jena took several deep breaths to try to calm down, but spots continued to dance before her eyes right before her legs gave out.

"Jena?"

She felt Harm's arms cinch around her, heard him call her name, and then he was carrying her off the dance floor. "I'm fine," she said quietly as he reached the table area outside the cordoned area. "I just got woozy."

Harm frowned down at her, his arms tight around her back and legs. "You almost passed out. That's not fine."

She shook her head. "I just need to sit down for a minute.

I haven't eaten since breakfast. Got too busy, and I guess it finally caught up with me."

Sighing, Harm headed for an empty table and set her down in the chair.

"You okay, Jena?" Hunter walked up, concern in his gaze as he set a water bottle on the table in front of her.

Jena picked up the water and managed a half smile. "I'm fine, Hunter. I just got lightheaded for a second."

Harm must've given Hunter some kind of look, because he nodded and backed off, saying, "Let me know if you need anything."

"You don't have to dance anymore," Harm said quietly once Hunter walked away.

Jena shook her head. "There's only twenty minutes left. I can deal."

Harm's lips pressed together, a determined look on his face. "I paid for the card. No more dancing."

Jena gestured toward Hunter, who was talking to his mom by the DJ table. "I have one more dance. I'll finish out the night."

"I'll buy Hunter's spot."

Jena jerked her gaze to his. "Don't you dare do that. I made a commitment and I'm going to fulfill it."

Harm's face settled into hard lines. "Do you ever think more than five minutes ahead, Jena? You're the most stubborn woman—" Cutting himself off, he stood and shoved his hands in his front pockets. "Make sure you don't fall flat on your face."

Jena kept her gaze on his belt buckle. She didn't need to look up at him. His tone told her he was mad at her. What's new? "I promise not to embarrass you, Harm."

She watched him walk away. The hard hit of his boots on the pavement reminded her of that day he'd stalked off after he'd regained his memory. Why did she keep pissing the man off? It seemed that's all she was good at lately. Sighing, she'd just returned her attention to the crowd when Hunter slid into the chair beside her.

"Are you sure you're all right?"

She nodded and sipped the water. "Thank you for the water."

He smiled. "Been waiting all night to dance with you. I've got to keep you hydrated."

A few minutes later, a teen in a red apron and matching baseball cap tapped her on the shoulder. "Are you Jena?"

She nodded. "Yes."

He quickly handed her a brown paper bag. "I was told to bring this right over."

Baffled, she took the bag and thanked him. After the boy ran off, she glanced inside and her mouth began to water. A chicken wrap and a bag of chips suddenly looked like a gourmet meal. Jena grabbed the bag of chips first. Their saltiness should help settle the nausea in her belly.

"Why didn't you tell me you were hungry?" Hunter asked, his brow furrowed.

She popped a chip in her mouth and chewed. "I didn't think about it until later. It's no biggie. I'll feel fine after I eat."

"Still, you should've told me," he grumbled.

Hunter let her eat in silence, and while she ate the rest of her food, Jena contemplated Harm's complexity. She really didn't understand him. She'd only gotten a glimpse of the lighter side of Harm tonight, yet he'd yanked that away so quickly, swinging back to the distant, judgy man she'd come to know these past few weeks. Sending her food had been nice of him, but why did she feel he'd done it because he felt obligated? Like he'd done when he bought her dance card? He didn't say he'd bought it because he *wanted* to dance with her.

Did she project an "I need to be rescued" vibe? Is that why he asked about her brother coming back? Was that comment about more than an indirect reminder about the land he still wanted to buy? Was it because, once her older brother returned, he wouldn't feel obligated to keep an eye on her? The last thing she wanted was to be anyone's obligation. She especially didn't want Harm to feel that way about her.

Maybe she'd been living in a dream world too long and she didn't have what it took to get Harm to open up. He might be the man of her dreams, but she was starting to realize that she wasn't the woman of his. And the thought depressed the hell out of her.

9

_____

"What the hell, Jena!"

Jena turned from touching up the shutter. She'd thought she was done with the shutters when she finished painting them yesterday, and she certainly wasn't dressed for painting in a sundress, but when she saw the spot she'd missed on her way out for an appointment with a realtor in town, she couldn't let it go. She'd rescheduled with the realtor for later in the afternoon, then pulled out the ladder and paint can.

She plucked the left ear bud from her ear, since Harm had yanked the right one out and turned off her phone sitting on the top of the ladder. She hadn't seen him in a couple of days, and now he stood on her porch yelling at her? Sighing, she stepped down from the ladder, then laid the paintbrush across the porch railing. "What have I done to tick you off now?"

"You're selling?" He scowled, then flung his arm toward

the drive. "And I had to find out when I drove past your property and saw the For Sale sign?"

"Calm down. My brother will be here this weekend, then we can draw up the paperwork. We're not going to sell it to anyone else. It'll all be yours soon enough."

He still looked angry. Why did he look angry? "I thought you weren't going to sell the house and land around it?" He gestured toward the shutters and flowerbeds. "You've just gotten it the way you wanted it. Why are you selling it now?"

She turned away and put the lid on the paint bucket. Tapping the lid down with a rubber mallet, she said, "Because I've been reminded enough times by enough people that it's time to grow up, and that I shouldn't let my flighty whims interfere with other people's lives. I guess believing in fairytales are a thing of my past." Taking a steadying breath, she faced him and kept her tone upbeat. "I've found a place in town that's closer to Dr. Macomb's practice. I start work next week, so you'll have plenty of room for more horses now. Make sure you put it to good use."

As she brushed past him, then headed for the barn, Harm's long strides quickly caught up to her. "You can't leave. You have responsibilities here: the horses, the house."

Jena slid a sideways glance his way. "You can take care of them; you've been doing so long before I came into the picture." Stopping, she pulled the house key from her pocket and held it out to him. "Here, you can have this back. I've got a spare at the house."

Harm frowned at the key in her hand as if it was going to light him on fire if he took it. "I don't think you're flighty, Jena. I know you work hard. I've seen your work ethic in how you've transformed Sally's house and with the horses."

His praise made her heart beat a little faster. "Thanks for saying that. It means a lot. And now you'll have a nice place to get away to if you want." Swinging the key on the ring, she said, "I take the apples and carrots out of the fridge a half hour before I give them to the horses. They like them just a little cold. I'll be back and forth while I'm meeting relators this week, so I'll need you to take care of Sally's horses if you don't mind."

When he took the key from her, she held his gaze. "I sincerely hope you find her, Harm."

His brow furrowed. "Who?"

She tilted her head. "The woman you'll be willing to take a risk for. I might've given up on fairytales, but I still believe in that." Forcing a smile, she walked away and entered the barn.

Harm was still standing where she left him when she came back out with a small bucket in her hand. Taking an apple from the bucket, she pushed herself to keep going, despite Harm's quiet presence, and moved to the fence where all four horses had trotted into position, waiting for her to give them their treat.

She'd fed three of the horses their apples, when Harm's deep voice sounded directly behind her.

"What about me, Jena?"

She paused, then lifted the apple to the last horse. "You?"

As the horse gobbled the apple up, Harm stepped so close she could feel his warmth spreading across her back. "Yeah, me. Are you going to leave me behind too? A month is a long time to deny myself the one woman who showed me that happy-ever-afters absolutely exist if I'd just trusted my damned heart from the start."

She jumped when his warm hands settled on her shoulders. "I've been a fool, Jena. I'm sorry I've been such a horse's ass, but you knocked the wind right the hell out of me. I would've come by sooner to talk, but one of my horses needed the vet's attention.

"Dancing with you the other night made me realize that the only way I'll ever feel settled again is if you say 'yes' to everything that happened between us that night." His fingers flexed slightly on her shoulders as he continued, "I need to hear you tell me that it was as real as it felt, because nothing has torn me up more than walking around thinking that the electric connection we shared was all in my head."

Jena's heart thumped hard and she blinked back tears. "It was real, Harm."

Harm bent close and whispered in her ear, "I've never felt as at peace as I did that night with you. I didn't know that's what true happiness felt like."

She pressed her face against his scruff, enjoying the feel of it against her skin. God, she missed that so much, along with his sexy, masculine smell. "If you realized all this, why did you get mad at me the other night at the dance?"

He kissed her temple and slid his arms around her waist, pulling her against his hard frame. "Because I was worried about you...and because I sure as hell didn't want to watch you dance in another man's arms. You were meant for me, Jena. Only me."

She let out a bubbly laugh. "Well, you wasted a good twenty minutes more of dancing because you were being so surly."

"You needed to eat." He pressed his lips to her neck, his voice gruff. "Stubborn woman." Cinching his arms tighter around her, he continued, "I've fallen in love with you, Jena Hudson. I want that night we shared to be reality for the rest of our lives, and I really hope you want that too."

Jena stilled. Was he asking her to marry him? Or was this as close as Harm could get to a commitment?

Before she could speak, he said, "Say yes. That's the only answer." Rubbing his nose along her jaw, his voice turned husky. "Do you know you have the sexiest voice? It makes me rock hard in record time."

As he pressed his erection against her backside, Jena couldn't help the smile that spread across her face. "And here I thought other parts of my body did that to you."

Harm expelled a low laugh, then slid his hands along her waist and upward until he cupped her breasts. "There are definitely parts of you I want to explore in excruciating detail, if for no other reason than to discover all the sounds you'll make when you're turned on."

To prove his point, he brushed his thumbs across her nipples through the linen material of her dress until the nubs pebbled. Jena squirmed against him and sighed in pleasure. She'd waited a long time to feel his hands touching her once more. The excited contentment she felt as he slid the straps of her dress down and exposed her breasts to the open air went way beyond craving a physical connection. It was about making a commitment. In her heart, she was already his.

When he rolled her sensitized nipples between his fingers and she moaned, arching back against him, Harm nipped at her ear, then nuzzled her neck. "Remember what I said about the next time we made love? And make no mistake, this *will* be making love—" His hands slid down her thighs. "I want to feel your hot, sweet skin sliding against every part of me.

When I ease inside you, I don't want anything between us, Jena."

She gulped back the flood of emotions raging through her. "Yes, I remember. I'm on the pill, so no condoms are necessary."

Her heart raced and the knots in her stomach unfurled, replaced with stomach-clenching anticipation as she felt him unbuttoning his pants behind her. Liquid heat pooled between her legs when he lifted her skirt.

"You have the sweetest ass," he said in a rough, you're-all-mine rumble at the same time he palmed her bare skin. "This g-string is a definite turn on."

When he traced his finger down the strap between her cheeks, she gasped, breathless. "I'm glad you approve."

At the same time he planted a kiss on her shoulder, he tugged on the edge of her underwear. "Thongs will be a requirement for the next fifty years or so. But for now," he pulled her panties down past her hips, "I don't want anything in my way."

As Jena stepped out of her underwear, the fierceness of his tone and permanency in his words struck a cord; she didn't need a piece of paper. She placed her hand over his on her breast, stilling his movements. "Are you sure this is what you want, Harm?" She couldn't handle it if he walked away from her again. It would tear her to pieces.

"I've never been more certain." He clasped his hand more firmly on her breast as he eased himself inside her. Filling her completely, possessively, he let out a groan. "I want a wife," he said, his voice rough with sincerity. "I want the two or three or a passel of kids. You made me want it all, Jena, but only with you." He withdrew and sank back home once more, causing her breath to hitch. Jena grasped the fence to keep herself upright as joy ricocheted through her. This wasn't a dream; he was actually asking her to marry him.

Placing his warm hands on hers, Harm locked their fingers together and draped his body over her back, his words like velvet sliding over her. "You didn't officially answer the question, so I'll be as clear as possible. Will you marry me, Jena? You have the power to make this fantasy a reality. And just in case you're hesitating at all, remember those three chances? I'll be happy to make the decision for you. As your prospective husband-to-be, I definitely think I know what's best for you."

His words warmed her heart. She let the tears she'd been holding back fall. "Yes, Harm. You've given me a reason to stay right where I am."

"Thank God." He expelled a breath.

She gave a watery laugh at his obvious relief.

"And by the way…" He dipped his head and lightly grazed his teeth along her neck. "Don't expect me to ever wear a condom again. I don't care how many kids we have. This feels too damn good to ever go back."

Jena shamelessly pushed against him. "Then finish what you started, cowboy."

"Happy to oblige, ma'am." He chuckled and slid his hands to her hips. Grasping her with loving strength, he withdrew, then plunged in, deep and hard.

Each time he joined with her felt more deeply emotional than the last; like they were connecting on a higher level. The tender way he held her, his body surrounding hers with warmth and support; it felt as if he was making love to her for the first time. In a way, he was, because this time their hearts and minds were in perfect sync.

The thought made Jena's heart skip several beats. She arched her back and contracted her muscles, smiling when his groan sounded both pained and pleased by her actions. But when he slid his hand down her hip, across her belly, then lower until he found her swollen flesh, her smile faltered and she gasped in sheer pleasure.

"I love you more than I could imagine possible." Rolling the sensitized bit of skin between his fingers, he continued, "Share with me, sweetheart, the first of many for the rest of our lives."

Jena's climax splintered through her in tingling waves, its sheer intensity making her shake all over.

As soon as she stopped gasping, Harm pulled out of her and immediately turned her around. Wrapping his hands around her waist, he lifted her up, then kissed her as he pulled her close and lowered her primed body down his erection.

"Mmmm, not one damn thing compares to this," he said in a hoarse voice as he slid fully inside her. Cupping her bare buttocks to protect her skin, he leaned against the fence and rolled his hips. Jena moaned, enjoying their intimate connection. Harm gave her a smile full of sin right before he withdrew and thrust back in, hard and fast. Jena gripped his shoulders tight and keened her pleasure, thrilled by his rough aggressiveness. She clasped her legs firmly around his waist and gyrated her hips, clenching her muscles around him, wanting him aching with as much need as she felt.

"Jena." He sounded wrecked, his body tensing under her.

"You ruined me for all other men that night. I love you,

you stubborn, beautiful man." She rocked against him once more to send him over the edge, but he held on, never letting his loving gaze leave hers as he kept up his rhythmic pace. Jena called his name as she flew apart with him, her body quivering all over from the body-melting sensations.

When their breathing settled and their heart rates slowed, Harm set her on the ground and silently pulled her back against his chest, wrapping his arms tight around her. She laid her head against his shoulder and watched the horses running in the lush, green pasture. "Um, you do know you only have two chances left, right?"

Harm's chest rumbled with laughter before he scooped her up and turned toward the house.

Jena squirmed in his arms and giggled as she tried to sound stern. "Put me down. We have work to do, Mr. Steele."

Harm's boots hit the porch and he glanced down at her, passionate determination in his gaze. "Yes, we do. Mrs. Steele-to-be. I suggest we start in the bedroom."

As he carried her over the threshold, Jena smiled and whispered, "Thank you, Great Aunt Sally."

10

The screen door banged shut behind Ty as he walked inside their great aunt's house, rubbing his hands together. "I'm so glad you're ready to sign and head back to Maryland," he said to Jena as she stood beside Harm in the kitchen, paperwork on the table beside them.

Jena smiled, then gestured to the rest of the house. "Don't you like what I've done to the place?"

Ty took a moment to glance around as he rolled up his shirt's sleeves. Jena smiled at his custom dress shirt. Her brother probably spent more on that shirt than she did on her entire outfit.

"Yeah, it looks nice, but I don't know why you bothered."

She chuckled, surprised he seemed oblivious to how close Harm was standing to her. "I *bothered*, because I'm staying, Ty."

Confusion flickered across her brother's handsome face. "But you said you're signing?"

She nodded. "I am, but you're going to have to stay a little longer. Maybe a week."

"What do you mean? It should take two seconds to close this deal." Ty looked ready to explode as he strode up to the table, his brow puckered. "I need to get back to Maryland, Jena."

Jena stepped forward and clasped his shoulders, kissing him on the cheek. "I need you to give me away at the wedding, silly. And of course, we'll fly Mom here."

As Ty's shocked gaze darted back and forth between Harm and her, she saw Harm fighting his laughter. Somehow he managed to keep his expression perfectly composed as he handed Ty a check for his half of Sally's property.

"Here's your check, Ty."

Taking the check, Ty gave her a stern look. "I remember how much you loved it here, so I can understand you wanting to stay for a while like we talked about, but there's no reason to rush into marriage."

When Harm narrowed his gaze and stiffened, Jena laughed.

"Fine, tell Mom we're dating then, but," she paused and caught Harm's gaze. Loving the heated look in his eyes, she reached out and clasped his hand. "It's going to be a short engagement."

"One month, no longer," Harm cut in, his matter-of-fact tone non-negotiable.

He sounded so dissatisfied, she grinned and glanced back to her brother. "Does that appease your brotherly worries?"

Ty's only response was to fold his arms and grunt.

Harm reached over and clapped Ty on the shoulder, a big

grin on his face. "You should come back to Texas and stay a while, Ty. You'll never want to leave either."

"Don't see that happening." Ty snorted as he stepped back and leaned against the kitchen counter, his stance relaxing somewhat.

Jena laughed, relieved that her brother had regained his sense of humor. "Oh, I don't know, Ty. Never say never. Texans have a way of growing on you."

Pulling her into his arms, Harm kissed the tip of her nose. "That we do, darlin'. That we do."

I HOPE you loved **HARM'S HUNGER** and will take the time to leave a review in the on-line store where you bought it. Keep flipping the pages to read an excerpt from book 2 in the **BAD IN BOOTS** series, **TY'S TEMPTA-TION** and following that, an excerpt for book 1, MISTER BLACK, in my *New York Times bestselling* **IN THE SHADOWS** contemporary romance series. And so you don't miss any new P.T. Michelle releases, be sure *to sign up for my newsletter here:* bit.ly/11tqAQN

TY'S TEMPTATION (BOOK 2) - EXCERPT

BAD IN BOOTS

"Is that your car?"

Ty finished paying for his soda and turned to the blond teen who'd tapped him on the shoulder. "What?"

The kid tilted his head toward the gas station parking lot. "Is that your red convertible?"

Ty unscrewed the cap and nodded, giving him an indulgent smile. He took a long swig and enjoyed the brief relief the cool beverage provided from the fall Texas heat. Letting out a sigh of satisfaction, he twisted the lid back on. "It's a rental, but it's my car while I'm visiting."

The sound of squealing tires screeched through the open door, and the boy smirked. "Looks like it's someone else's car now."

Ty jerked his gaze to the parking lot in time to see the taillights of his rented sports car shoot into traffic. His heart raced and anger quickly slammed to the surface. "Why didn't you say something sooner?"

The boy shrugged as he put his candy bar on the counter. "Hey, I just saw him get into the convertible. I didn't know if the guy was with you or not."

Ty mentally counted to ten while he jangled his keys in

front of the kid. "Seeing him hotwire my car didn't clue you in?"

The teenager handed his money to the young female cashier, who was listening to their conversation with avid interest. Peeling away the wrapper, he took a bite out of his candy bar. The strong smell of peanuts and chocolate drifted Ty's way as the boy spoke, "Maybe you shouldn't have left your top down."

Ty drove along the tree-lined dirt road that led to his Great-Aunt Sally's Double D ranch. Gravel crunched under his tires as he rolled to a halt in the driveway in front of the small one-story house. He climbed out of the cramped, two-seater sports car and grimaced, pressing his palm against his stiff spine. *That'll teach me to ask for the first available convertible.* Pulling his cell from his pocket, he leaned on the car's hood and dialed Jena's number.

"It's about time, Ty!"

"Heya, Sis. I'm at the Double D. Thanks for sending the key."

"Where have you been? I tried your cell, but you must've left it turned off. I expected you to come by Steele Way and have lunch with us hours ago. We've held off the wedding for a couple of months now while you finished your project...and you take your sweet time getting here? I want you to see Harm's ranch and spend some time getting to know my fiancé."

"That 'project' was a eight-million-dollar, state-of-the-art building, Jena. It raised Hudson & Shannon's reputation in the architectural community several notches." Ty rubbed the back of his neck, feeling the weight of the three-hour police interview and annoying paperwork with the car rental agency starting to take its toll. "I'll see you tomorrow, bright and early. Let's just say I've had a hell of a day. I want to hit the hay early tonight."

"Is everything all right?"

He ran a hand through his hair and down the five o'clock shadow on his jaw, chuckling. "Yeah. Apparently the Hudsons don't have the best of luck with rental cars."

"Oh no! Did your car die on you, too?"

"Worse. It was stolen."

"You're kidding me!"

Ty gave a tired sigh. "I wish I were."

"I'm so sorry. Do you need us to come get you?"

"No, I've got another car, but I'll see you tomorrow as promised."

"Okay. Get some rest."

Ty put his phone away and opened the car door to pull out his suitcase. The empty backseat was a jarring reminder his suitcase was still in the stolen car, including his custom made suit. "I hope he's too short for my clothes," he grumbled as he headed for the front door.

As soon as he walked inside, Ty noticed two things—Jena kept her promise to have the place ready for him, and he couldn't get enough of the smell permeating the room. Cinnamon and apples.

Glancing to the left of the entryway to the kitchen, he grinned when he saw a pie sitting on the stove. His sister knew how much he loved apple pie. The kitchen flowed right into the living room, where he and Jena had spent many hours playing card games with their great-aunt and toasting marshmallows in the stone fireplace. A big picture window took up the wall straight ahead of him. The door farthest away opened to the only bedroom. The door next to it led to a two-way bathroom that served as the bedroom and guest bathroom.

When his attention circled back to the small, efficient kitchen, with its wooden table and four mission-style chairs, he smiled in memory of his and Jena's past summer visits with their great-aunt. He didn't even mind that he spent his nights sleeping on a foldout cot so Jena could have the sofa bed.

You'd better wash those hands and freshen up before you dare to sit at my table. His aunt's stern, but loving voice entered his head as if it were yesterday and not twenty years since he'd last seen her.

"I miss your spunky self, Aunt Sal," he murmured, regretting he didn't get a chance to see her before she passed away.

Ty started toward the bathroom, and as he walked past the end table next to the couch, he noticed the paring knife and plate his sister had forgotten to take back to the kitchen. Shaking his head, he chuckled. Some things never changed. Growing up, Jena had always forgotten to put her dishes away.

As soon as he put his hand on the bathroom's doorknob, the door jerked open. A tall woman, wearing nothing but a fluffy white towel, walked out of the bathroom.

"Aaaaahh!" She took a step back, her mouth a tiny "O" of shock.

Ty raised his hands. "Hey, I—"

Before he had a chance to finish, she ripped off the towel, then threw the cloth over his head, blocking his view.

Heart racing from the unexpected scenario, Ty reached to grab the towel from his face. A jolting blow to the back of his knees caused his legs to buckle. Another hit behind his ankles sent his feet flying. As he landed flat on his back, air whooshed out of his lungs. *What the hell?* Still reeling, he heard a loud crash on the floor. Adrenaline thrummed through him as he started to remove the towel, but instead of finding freedom, his wrists, then his ankles were quickly bound with something thin yet strong.

When the towel flew off his face, Ty rolled over ceramic shards on the wood floor as he struggled against what appeared to be an electrical cord binding.

The woman leaned over him. One hand clutched the towel to her breasts and the other held a paring knife pointed at his throat. "Move another inch and you'll find out the hard way I'm not afraid to stick you like the trussed-up pig you are." Straightening, she backed away, her movements slow and cautious.

Water dripped from her hair onto the delicate slope of her shoulders, disappearing in the valley between her breasts. Now that she'd stopped moving, he realized her hair was a light color. Strawberry-blonde maybe?

Obviously he'd scared the shit out of her. Despite the misunderstanding, Ty was impressed by her quick reflexes and instinctive defensive responses.

He met her angry gaze and stared. She had the most unusual, mesmerizing eyes, robin's-egg blue, flecked with shades of gold and brown. "I believe you're trespassing," he said in a calm voice.

"*I'm* trespassing." She frowned. "You're the one who's trespassing. I was invited."

Ty raised an eyebrow. "So was I."

Her delicate golden brows drew together. "By whom?"

"By my sister. She owns this place."

"Jena's your sister?"

Ty smiled at the squeak in her voice. The pink tinge that colored her cheeks was so sincere.

He nodded. "I'm Ty Hudson."

"Oh, my God! I'm so sorry." Setting the knife on the plate on the end table, she turned her back to wrap the towel around herself.

Ty grinned at the brief glimpse he got of her perfect ass.

Turning back, she kneeled next to him. As she untied the electrical cord from around his ankles, she said, "Harm invited me to stay here."

Anger sliced through him. "Harm?" It had only been two months since Harm asked Jena to marry him. The man better not have a woman on the side or he would have to kill the bastard!

His expression must've reflected his thoughts, because she quickly explained, "Harm had problems with one of Sally's horses. With the wedding days away and his attention otherwise occupied, I volunteered to stay here to keep an eye on the mare and make sure she's healing fine."

As she leaned over him to undo the knot at his wrists, water dripped onto his dress shirt. Not that he cared. He was too busy enjoying the scent teasing his nostrils—cinnamon and vanilla. Damn, she smelled good. And here he thought cinnamon and apples smelled like heaven. *Her* scent had just blown that theory to smithereens. He inhaled once, twice, three times, drinking in her intoxicating aroma.

She looked at him, concern in her gaze. "Are you okay? Did I tie you too tight?"

When the last of the cord slid off him, she started to pull away. Ty grabbed her wrist. Grinning, he lowered his voice. "You're welcome to tie me up anytime you want."

Color bloomed on her cheeks once more, making him realize he hadn't seen such a genuine reaction in a woman in a very long time. His suspicions kicked in. Full force. She had to be around twenty-five or so. No way she was *that* innocent.

Without responding, she used his hold on her wrist to help pull him to his feet.

Once they stood facing one another, Ty's grip loosened, yet he still didn't want to release her. Despite the warning bells clanging in his head, he felt a sudden urge to learn everything about her. "You never told me your name."

Evan's heart raced and electricity hummed when he slid his fingers slowly down her wrist, then traced his thumb along her palm.

Concentrating on answering, instead of the intense physical awareness he ignited, helped her regain focus. "I'm Evan Masters."

"Nice to meet you, Miss. Masters." Ty lifted her left hand and turned it over, planting a kiss on her open palm.

Whether he meant it or not, his kiss had felt so intimate, her stomach flip-flopped. Evan's gaze landed on his short, silky dark hair, skimmed the starched blue cotton shirt that stretched across broad shoulders, then moved to his gray dress slacks and Italian leather shoes. The man's impeccable, expensive clothes were a stark contrast to the worn jeans and casual tank top that awaited her on the bed in the bedroom.

"Um, I hope we can start over. That wasn't my best first impression."

His vivid green gaze held a dark, intense look before his eyebrows rose in amusement. "At least I'm now versed in how well you can defend yourself."

She gave a sheepish smile. "My dad made sure I knew how to take care of myself."

Ty glanced at the gutted table lamp. Bits of blue ceramic scattered across the floor and the ripped-out electrical cord now lay in an innocent tangle on the floor. "I might've gotten knocked off my feet and all tied up, but I think the lamp got the worse of it."

Evan glanced at the lamp pieces and grimaced. "Looks like I'll be buying Jena a new lamp."

When Ty chuckled, she felt inordinately pleased that she had made him smile. For the first time in her life, a man grabbed her rapt attention. Correction...this particular man made her tingle and ache everywhere. And this reaction was triggered by nothing more than a complimentary comment and a blatant sexy gaze. *My God, what would he be like when he really turned on the charm?*

Check out Ty's Temptation

MISTER BLACK - EXCERPT

IN THE SHADOWS SERIES

Check out a brief excerpt from book one, MISTER BLACK, *in my* **New York Times** *and* **USA Today** *best selling contemporary romance* **IN THE SHADOWS** *series.*

Straightening, Sebastian takes off his belt and shirt. His breathing saws in and out as he stares down at me for a beat before removing his mask. I'm glad to know I'm not the only one affected. The outline of his broad shoulders and hard, fit body make me want to explore every dip and hollow with my tongue. I'm sad that it's too dark to see more than bits of light play on his face from trees moving in the wind outside, but that means he can't really see mine either.

I reach up and remove my mask. I want to kiss him without it in the way. I don't want anything between us. We'll just hide in the shadows instead.

"Your name," he says, his tone demanding compliance.

I pull my dress over my head, tossing it to him.

My answer.

He crushes the material in a tight fist, then drops it to the floor. Reaching for my ankles, he encircles them, fingers flexing on my skin. Distant lightning flashes, briefly highlighting the top half of his face. The room goes dark again, and all I can picture is the near feral look in his amazing eyes as he tugs me toward him with a powerful jerk, his tone gravelly and full of want. "Then I'll just call you *Mine*."

When he runs his hands up the inside of my thighs, pressing them to the bed with a quiet order, "Keep them here," I comply, eager anticipation curling in my belly. I'm exposed, but he's already seen the ugliest side of me. When I was raw and at my weakest. He just doesn't know it.

Be sure to check out Mister Black

ACKNOWLEDGEMENTS

To my beta readers, Joey Berube and Magen Chambers, thank you so much for your amazing support of my work and for providing great feedback on HARM'S HUNGER. You've helped make it a better story!

OTHER BOOKS BY P.T. MICHELLE

**In the Shadows
(Contemporary Romance, 18+)**
Mister Black (Book 1 - Talia & Sebastian)
Scarlett Red (Book 2 - Talia & Sebastian)
Blackest Red (Book 3 - Talia & Sebastian)
Gold Shimmer (Book 4 - Cass & Calder)
Steel Rush (Book 5 - Cass & Calder)
Black Platinum (Book 6 - Talia & Sebastian)
Reddest Black (Book 7 - Talia & Sebastian) - Late Fall 2017

**Brightest Kind of Darkness Series
(YA/New Adult Paranormal Romance, 16+)**
Ethan (Prequel)
Brightest Kind of Darkness (Book 1)
Lucid (Book 2)
Destiny (Book 3)
Desire (Book 4)
Awaken (Book 5)

**Other works by P.T. Michelle writing as Patrice
Michelle**

**Bad in Boots series
(Contemporary Romance, 18+)**
Harm's Hunger
Ty's Temptation
Colt's Choice
Josh's Justice

**Kendrian Vampires series
(Paranormal Romance, 18+)**
A Taste for Passion
A Taste for Revenge
A Taste for Control

Stay up-to-date on her latest releases:

Join P.T's Newsletter:
http://bit.ly/11tqAQN

Visit P.T. :

Website: http://www.ptmichelle.com
Twitter: https://twitter.com/PT_Michelle
Facebook: https://www.facebook.com/PTMichelleAuthor
Instagram: http://instagram.com/p.t.michelle
Goodreads:
http://www.goodreads.com/author/show/4862274.P_T_Mic
helle

P.T. Michelle's Facebook Readers' Group:
https://www.facebook.com/groups/PTMichelleReadersGroup/

ABOUT THE AUTHOR

P.T. Michelle is the *NEW YORK TIMES, USA TODAY*, and International Bestselling author of the New Adult contemporary romance series IN THE SHADOWS, the YA/New Adult crossover series BRIGHTEST KIND OF DARKNESS, and the romance series: BAD IN BOOTS, KENDRIAN VAMPIRES and SCIONS (listed under Patrice Michelle). She keeps a spiral notepad with her at all times, even on her nightstand. When P.T. isn't writing, she can usually be found reading or taking pictures of landscapes, sunsets and anything beautiful or odd in nature.

   To learn when the next P.T. Michelle book will release, join P.T.'s free newsletter http://bit.ly/11tqAQN

Follow P.T. Michelle

www.ptmichelle.com

CPSIA information can be obtained
at www.ICGtesting.com
Printed in the USA
LVHW090046250520
656510LV00002B/417